PUNCH, PASTRIES, AND POISON

A Cape Bay Cafe Mystery Book 10

HARPER LIN

Chapter 1

LATE SPRING IS my favorite time of year in Cape Bay. The icy chill of Massachusetts winter is finally out of the air, the trees are back in full leaf, and the humidity and tourist throngs haven't yet descended on the coast. The feeling is glorious, and I want to spend every second of every day outdoors, soaking it up.

So, naturally, instead of doing that, I was holed up in the back room of Antonia's, sorting through invoices and poring over resumes.

After nearly a year as sole proprietor of the coffee shop my grandparents had opened sixty-some-odd years ago when they'd first arrived here from Italy, I was ready to make some changes. Okay, maybe I wasn't actually ready to make them, but I'd found myself increasingly feeling like it was time to change, particularly to bring on new staff.

Antonia's had been running on a staff of five for a year, since my late mother—the café's previous owner—had hired two high school students on shortly before her death. That had been enough to get by, but I didn't want to just get by. I wanted to flourish. And with tourist season coming, flourishing meant I needed some more help.

I looked down again at the resume in front of me. Persephone Phillips. She didn't have much experience, but I doubted that Becky and Amanda —my high school girls—had much before starting, either, and in any case, I mostly wanted the new person to help with taking orders, running them out to tables, and keeping the place clean. Not exactly rocket science.

I glanced up at the clock on the wall. Persephone should have been here by now. Running late was not exactly the kind of first impression I'd been hoping she'd make.

With a sigh, I picked up the stack of new resumes and applications from the corner of the little table that passed as a desk in the café's back room. I looked down at the first one. Bradford Bradenton Bradshaw IV. He had a master's degree

2

in finance and a few years of experience working on Wall Street. Why on earth was he applying at my little coffee shop? Did he think I was hiring for a finance manager instead of a cashier? If I was, it would be for probably the least interesting finance job ever, since I had no problem keeping up with our books even though I was a communications major in school.

The next applicant was a girl who had just turned fourteen the week before—she had it written on her application and mentioned it to me when she dropped it off—whose parents had no doubt urged her to go ahead and find a summer job before they were all taken.

I wasn't completely opposed to hiring a fourteen-year-old. If she was a good fit, I could hope to have her for four good years before she graduated high school. Fourteen—barely fourteen—just seemed so young. I looked back down at the application she'd turned in and gasped when I realized that she hadn't even started high school yet. She was still in middle school! I reminded myself that her education level had no bearing on her ability to take an order, and I flipped her application over on top of Bradford Bradenton Bradshaw IV's in the Maybe pile. Middle school!

I was still shaking my head when Sammy—my café manager and general right-hand woman—poked her head through the doorway.

"Sammy, you need to look at the applications I got yesterday." I grabbed Bradford Bradenton Bradshaw IV and the middle-schooler's papers from the pile and held them out to her.

"I'd love to"—she held out a single finger—"but your interview is here."

I glanced up at the clock. She was almost ten minutes late. That irked me, but I didn't think it was reason enough to dismiss her without even speaking to her. Maybe she'd gotten stuck in traffic or been getting in her car when she realized her blouse had a big grease stain from the pizza she'd dropped on it last time she wore it. Sometimes those didn't come out in the wash. It happened. I knew from experience.

"What do you think of her?" I asked. "Does she seem like she'd be a good fit?"

Sammy shrugged. "She just came in and said she was here for her interview. I didn't really talk to her."

"Did she apologize for being late?"

Sammy gave me a sympathetic smile.

"Nobody's perfect, Fran. No matter how much you'd like them to be."

I resisted the urge to point out that I couldn't imagine having a more perfect employee than her and stood up from my chair. "Well, hopefully she's a good fit, because I'm tired of looking at resumes."

I followed Sammy out in the café and looked across the counter at the girl she pointed out.

My heart sank.

I was pretty sure a pizza stain on her blouse wasn't the cause of her lateness. A cat attack seemed more likely. Or a vigorous sword fight.

Under certain circumstances, I could have forgiven her for wearing a T-shirt and jeans to an interview—some people just didn't know better, and this place was just a coffee shop, after all. The holes were what really got me. I could see at least five in the baggy black T-shirt, one of which was a slash across her abdomen that left a gaping swath of her midriff exposed.

Her acid-washed jeans were similarly scattered with holes. If they hadn't somehow been still attached to her, I would have thought she ran them through a shredder.

I looked at Sammy imploringly, silently begging her to tell me I was looking at the wrong girl.

Instead, she leaned over and said quietly in my ear, "It's the fashion." She inclined her head slightly towards a group of college-aged girls who had set up camp at one of the tables with their laptops, a stack of pastries, and their lattes. Their clothes, too, looked like they'd spent some time at the mercy of a razor.

I sighed and resolved myself to ignoring her outfit. And her lateness. And her hair needing a visit with a comb. I took one more look at Sammy, hoping she'd finally admit that Persephone was a no-show, then walked around the counter to the girl. "Hi, Persephone?" I gave her a warm smile and stuck out my hand. "I'm Fran. It's a pleasure to meet you."

She stared down at my hand before slowly taking it, if you could call what she did taking it. It was more like she slipped her hand limply into mine and allowed me to attempt to shake it. The second I released it, she pulled it back and wiped it on her jeans.

I clenched my teeth and forced myself to keep smiling. "Why don't you follow me to the back and we can get started?" I turned and headed for the back, catching Sammy's eye on the way. I widened my eyes, knowing she'd caught every second of the awkward greeting and attempt at a handshake. She grinned back at me but didn't make any movement to let me know that this was an elaborate joke, which I was still wishing it was.

My hopes momentarily dashed, I led Persephone to the back, pulled up a chair opposite mine, and sat down, gesturing for her to do the same.

She peered down at it, made a face, brushed off whatever invisible dirt she thought she saw, and sat down, perching on the very edge of the chair.

I gritted my teeth some more, then smiled big. "So, Persephone, what makes you want to work here at Antonia's?"

I listened to the seconds literally tick away on the little wall clock above my computer. It slowly dawned on me that she hadn't spoken at all yet. *Could* she speak? We had arranged the interview by email, so she hadn't had to speak then. But wouldn't she have mentioned it? I picked up her application in case she'd written it down there and I just hadn't noticed. "Um, do we—" I started, wondering if we needed to work out another means of communication. Before I could finish my sentence, she finally spoke up.

"It's Ephy."

I looked up at her, trying to figure out what on earth she'd just said. "I'm sorry?"

"It's Ephy," she repeated in a monotone. "You keep calling me Persephone, but no one calls me that."

I forced a smile as I glanced down at the empty spot on the application labeled "nickname." I held my pen over it. "E-F?"

She stared at me.

I held back a sigh.

"P-H."

I smiled and nodded. "I?"

She cocked her head to the side with an expression like she thought I was talking nonsense.

"E-P-H-I?" I enunciated each letter.

She heaved a sigh and rolled her eyes. "Why?"

I could feel my smile getting more patronizing by the second. I clenched the pen tighter in my fingers. "I just want to be able to spell your name correctly."

Again with her condescending look. I resisted the urge to stand up and show her straight to the door. "So, you spell it E-P-H-I?"

"Why?" she asked again, sounding even more irritable.

I was halfway to standing when it clicked. I sank

back down in my chair, my face feeling like it was on fire, and wrote down the letter Y at the end of her name. She hadn't been being difficult at all. She was spelling her name just as I asked. No wonder she was looking at me like I'd lost my mind. "Oh, of course, sorry about that." I smiled again, deciding I was going to have a new attitude towards her and the interview. "So, what makes you want to work here?"

"I, like, really like coffee and stuff?"

So much for the new attitude. "Have you ever used a professional-grade espresso machine?"

"Yeah?"

"What kind?"

She rattled off a list of high-end espresso machines, some of which even I hadn't even used.

I was surprised. I looked again at her resume, which definitely didn't list any coffee shop experience. "Have you worked in a coffee shop before?"

She shrugged as her eyes wandered the room. "Just filling in for people? Like, my friends and stuff?"

I nodded, but I was skeptical. Hiring someone who needed to be taught how to use the machine from the bottom up would give me more work to do, not less. And if she needed to learn that from scratch, I'd probably have to teach her how to make all the drinks too. Between her attitude and her lack of experience, it wasn't looking good for her. But I was afraid I wasn't giving her a fair chance. I'd already leapt to a conclusion about her once. I'd never been responsible for hiring before, and I didn't want to screw it up. I needed help—good help—in the café, and I wouldn't get it by cutting interviews off after a couple of questions.

I took a deep breath and, despite my better judgement, plowed ahead.

Chapter 2

THE REST of the interview actually wasn't a disaster. Not completely anyway. Her answers to my questions always seemed to end in a question mark, but they were reasonable. And she actually had a good response to how she would handle a crowded café with refills, orders, and dirty tables all needing attention. But as I led her out to the espresso machine to test out the skills I was highly skeptical she had, I didn't think she was going to get the job. "Here you go." I waved at the machine with all its dials and knobs and gauges. "Make me whatever you want."

She nodded silently as she looked it over. She touched a couple of the dials but didn't change them. Then she peeked at the grounds in the portafilter, waving her hand over them and sniffing. "Where are your beans?" she asked, still examining the machine.

"Grounds are right there." I gestured at the airtight jar beside the drip coffee maker. It was a test. She might have spent a little time in a coffee shop, and she might have even pulled espresso shots. But plenty of people could dump beans into an automatic espresso machine and pull a lever or two to get coffee out. I wanted to see what else she knew.

She wrinkled her nose. "The beans for espresso?"

I held back the smile that desperately wanted to creep across my face. "Behind you."

She turned around and picked up one. "You roast your own, right? When did you do these?"

"Yes. Those are from this morning."

She shook her head and put the bag down. "Do you have any from, like, yesterday? Like, yesterday morning?"

My smile broke through. I nodded in the direction of the bags of beans farther down the counter.

Ephy picked up one of the older bags and held it to her nose. "What's the blend?"

"Single-origin Kona. They have labels on the bottom."

She flipped the bag over and read the label before setting the bag down. She examined several other bags and then came back to the Hawaiian. "Grinder?"

I pointed it out with my stomach clenched. Those Kona beans were the most expensive ones we had in stock. They were so precious to me, I had roasted them myself the day before instead of letting Sammy handle it like she did most of the beans. I was hesitant to let her use them, even though it was only a small bag. What if she ruined them? What if she used the whole bag and didn't even make a useable grind? I pressed my nails into the palms of my hands and didn't say a word.

Ephy opened the bag and sniffed it, closing her eyes. She nodded and poured the beans into the grinder—not all of them but more than she needed to. I held my breath. If she ground them the way you typically would a Kona, they would be all wrong for espresso. I couldn't believe how nervous I was, both for her and for my precious beans.

Fortunately for both the coffee and me, she got the perfect grind then turned back to the semi-automatic espresso machine. She loaded up the basket with the fresh grounds then popped it into the machine. With smooth movements, she adjusted everything to her liking and pulled a shot. Instead of handing it to me, she took a sip and nodded. Then she pulled two more shots in quick succession. She added milk to one of the cups, giving her wrist a slight flick, then put them both on the counter in front of me.

"A straight shot and a flat white. I wanted you to be able to get the true flavor of the espresso, and then I figured you'd want to see my milk skills, so I made the flat white. It's, like, really simple, so you can still taste the bean, you know? It's kind of chocolatey, and that's, like, one of the highlights of Kona."

I blinked at her for a few seconds, mildly impressed with her knowledge of the bean's flavor profile, before I remembered that the taste of the espresso mattered a lot more than her book knowledge of coffee. She could have the technical aspects of making espresso down pat and still fail miserably in her execution. Kind of like my boyfriend Matt and pretty much any sport—he loved them all and knew everything about all of them but couldn't play for the life of him.

I picked up the flat white first, deliberately

leaving the shot for later. That flick of her wrist as she poured in the milk had been her decorating the drink with a delicate, pretty heart. It was just what I liked to see. Yet again, I reminded myself that, no matter how much I liked a pretty drink, the taste was what really mattered. I brought the cup towards my nose and sniffed it. The aroma was perfect and set my mouth watering, but I forced myself to be patient. I tipped the cup toward me and gave it the slightest swirl so I could get a better look at the color and consistency. It was a beautiful dark caramel. So far, a drink that I would be proud to have made myself.

I finally brought the cup to my lips, took a sip, and swished the coffee around my mouth for a few seconds before swallowing. The taste was near-heavenly, everything I looked for in a good cup of Kona—bright and fruity with a touch of acid and a hint of chocolate. I'd already seen enough to feel confident that I understood her coffee skills, but I still wanted to follow through on the final test—the espresso.

As much as I wanted to finish the flat white, I put it down and looked at the small cup still sitting on the counter. "How long do you think that's been sitting there?"

Ephy shrugged.

"A minute or so, you think?"

Her eyes turned down to the cup then back to me. She shrugged again.

"You think that's okay? Kind of a while for an espresso, don't you think?" This was also a test. There was a school of thought that you couldn't leave a shot of espresso sitting for more than thirty seconds before it turned irretrievably bitter. I thought that was ridiculous. A good bean, properly roasted and properly brewed, should still taste just as delicious cold as it did fresh out of the machine. In fact, as far as I was concerned, if it didn't taste good cold, it hadn't actually been good fresh either.

To my surprise, Ephy didn't shrug this time. "No, that's dumb. I hate when people say that. Good espresso is good espresso. You could leave that sitting there until tomorrow, and it would still taste good."

I fought back a smile. "Well, I think that would be a health code violation, but I see your point." I picked up the espresso. "And I agree." I took a quick sip and then slugged the whole thing back. It was every bit as good as I'd expected it to be.

So now I had a decision to make. Ephy's personality and look weren't exactly what I'd had in mind when I set out to find someone new for the café, but her coffee-making skills were top-notch, and I'd hardly have to train her at all. Unless I wanted to try to train her to smile, but I wasn't sure that would be a successful endeavor.

I glanced around the café. Sammy was making the rounds with the coffee pot, offering refills and chatting up the regulars. I wished I could ask her opinion, but she'd barely exchanged two words with Ephy. Even if I asked, she'd refuse, saying she hadn't spent enough time with her to be fair. It was one of Sammy's best—and occasionally most frustrating—qualities.

I sighed and leaned back against the counter, folding my arms across my chest while Ephy examined her fingernails and picked at the already chipped polish. "You can't do that if I hire you," I snapped.

She raised her eyes to me, not seeming to be at all put off by my comment or my tone. If anything, she seemed confused. "Do what? Make good coffee?"

I barely stopped my eyes from rolling. I could easily regret hiring this girl within thirty minutes of her first shift starting. "Pick at your nail polish. In fact, I don't want you coming in with chipped nail polish at all. Your nails should be bare or have a full coat."

She shrugged yet again and shoved her hands in her pockets.

"And no holes in your clothes. And pull your hair back."

One of her shoulders twitched, but that was all.

I took a deep breath and wondered if I was crazy to even consider hiring her.

The bell over the café door jingled, and I turned to see a group of twenty or so women pouring in, all clad in matching teal T-shirts emblazoned with Brookline Babes Beach Bonanza across their chests. Sammy looked up from where she was schmoozing with a small group crowded around a smaller table with their laptops. She went wide-eyed. Even without our regular customers, we were going to be slammed for at least the next half hour with that size group. And that was if they got their drinks to go. If they stayed, we'd be packed for at least an hour, maybe more.

I turned back to Ephy. "Tell you what. You stay here and help us out with this group, and if you do a good job, you're hired. I'll pay you either way."

For some reason, I expected a little enthusiasm from her about my offer, but all I got was a cool

"Sure." She fished a hair tie out from the stack of cords and bangles on her wrist and pulled back her thick mane of wavy, purple-tinged black hair.

I caught Sammy's eye as she hurried around the counter and dropped the coffee pot back on its warmer. "Sammy, this is Ephy. She's going to help us out with this group." I turned to Ephy. "Do whatever Sammy says."

Ephy nodded from the sink, where she was already washing her hands. Maybe she wouldn't be so bad after all. The next couple of hours would give me my answer.

I turned to the first customer, who was already standing at the register, and smiled. "Hi, welcome to Antonia's. What can I get for you today?"

She stared up at Sammy's handwritten menu on the chalkboard hanging behind the counter. "Uhh-hh." She sighed. "I never know what to get. I like the drinks that have all that whipped cream and chocolate sauce and stuff. What's a macchiato? Is that something I'd like? That's a fun name! Match-ee-ahh-toe." She turned around and giggled at the rest of her group.

I sighed. This was going to be an even better test for Ephy than I thought.

Chapter 3

THREE DAYS LATER, I was actually happy that I'd decided to hire Ephy—mostly. She was, as I'd already learned, a wiz at coffee, and she'd surprised me by knowing a thing or two about baking as well. Her first scheduled shift, she'd come in—appropriately dressed and groomed, no less—and spotted a tray of shortbread cookies waiting to go in the oven. She peered at them for long enough that I was about to tell her what they were and maybe even what a cookie was based on the forehead wrinkles that marred her otherwise impeccable complexion. But just as I opened my mouth, she looked up at me.

"Shortbread, right?"

I nodded.

"Do you use cornstarch in them?"

"Nope. Just butter, flour, and sugar. It's really easy, actually—there's a ratio—"

She cut me off. "My grandma used cornstarch. It's the best way to do it. Makes the cookie melt in your mouth. You should try it sometime." She cast a disdainful look at the cornstarch-free cookies on the tray and walked away towards the espresso machine.

I went after her out of some combination of self-punishment and curiosity. "So did your grandmother bake a lot?"

She nodded as she checked over the machine. She used slightly different settings than the ones I liked, but I couldn't argue with her results. In the couple of hours she'd worked with us after her interview, she'd earned raves from the customers. Not that the teal-shirted Brookline Babes were coffee connoisseurs, but they were pleased with their drinks, and so were the regulars she served.

"Did you bake with her?" I was trying to be friendly, but I was also trying to figure out if she'd be interested in working on the baking side of things as well.

"I worked in her shop for a while."

"Her shop?"

She had moved on to sniffing bags of beans. They were pretty airtight, so I didn't know what she was smelling, but she seemed to have a plan, so I left it alone.

"Yeah," she said. "She had a bake shop up in Maine. I helped out until she decided to retire and sold it to some yuppie couple who took all the gluten and sugar out of everything and stopped using ingredients from more than a hundred miles away, which is fine, you know, but it's not what people go to a bake shop for, especially since they didn't even sell coffee anymore 'cause it's from too far away, just some dandelion tea crap they harvested from a field somewhere because they told the farmer they'd do it for free if they could keep the product. And, I mean, who wouldn't take that deal, you know? They weeded his freaking field for free so they could get some weeds to make tea out of. And not even, like, actual weed, 'cause that might be good, but literal weeds from the ground, like the kind that kids make wishes on. Anyway, they're only open, like, two hours a day now, and there's only this one guy named Jim who ever comes in to drink their weed juice and eat their mashed-up blueberries and potatoes, because what the hell else grows in Maine? I don't even know how they stay in business. I think their family gives them money or something."

I stood in silence for a minute, digesting the torrent of words that had just poured out of her mouth. It was easily the most I'd heard her say in one go, and I suspected that if I counted up all the words I'd ever heard her say, that speech would have accounted for more than half. Still, I was glad she was showing some passion about something and fascinated that her expression hadn't so much as flickered the entire time. Her face had remained completely impassive the entire time, and she hadn't missed a beat in her inspection of the beans.

"Wow," I said. "That sounds terrible. I'd hate for something like that to happen to Antonia's."

The Ephy shrug returned. "If they want to ruin a good business, that's on them. Doesn't bother me. They paid my grandma well."

And that was that. She finally decided on a bag of beans—the first one she'd sniffed, actually—grabbed it, and went over to the espresso machine like we hadn't just been having a conversation. I had a feeling it was something I'd just have to get used to if I was going to keep her around, which I planned to. Her personality may not have been stellar, but her coffee was, and besides, we needed the help.

Fortunately, she somehow managed to mostly get along with most of the staff and customers. She was polite but not warm, and she kept her head down and did her job. She showed up close to on time—punctuality was another of her weak spots— didn't mind staying a few minutes late, and did as she was told. She even got me to try her grand-mother's shortbread recipe, which, I had to admit, was melt-in-your-mouth delicious. So, for the most part, I felt like I made the right call in hiring her.

Her third day, I even trusted her enough to leave her out front while I went in the back to check our stock levels and see what we needed to reorder. Napkins, probably. It was always napkins.

I'd been back there for about twenty minutes when Ephy appeared out of thin air beside me, as if she'd teleported. I'd even been facing the door and hadn't seen or heard her coming until I looked up from my clipboard and saw her standing there stone-faced in front of me. I jumped and dropped my clipboard. "Ephy! You startled me!"

"Some guy's here to see you?"

I bent down and grabbed the clipboard. "Who is it?"

She shrugged.

I took a deep breath. If I was going to keep her, I'd just have to accept that I would periodically have to explain to her how I wanted her to behave in situations where someone else would have already known. Ephy either didn't know or didn't care, and I'd just have to accept and correct that. "Next time, ask their name before you come back to get me, okay?"

She shrugged, and I had no idea whether she would do it or not.

I jotted down the number of napkins I thought we needed to order—never enough, even when I ordered twice as many—and laid the clipboard on the desk on my way out into the café. The first man I laid eyes on was my old friend Mike Stanton, who was just walking through the door. Instinctively, I went straight for the coffee pot, dumped it, and started a new batch. "One minute," I mouthed in his direction. Mike always ordered the same thing —a large black coffee to go—so I'd gotten in the habit of starting a fresh pot as soon as I saw him. With as much coffee as he drank, the man would have single-handedly kept us in business if he paid for any of it, but police officers and firefighters had eaten for free at our coffee shop since my grandparents' days, and Mike was the lead—and only—detective in the Cape Bay police department. Luckily, he kept his orders simple, so his coffee habit didn't bankrupt me either.

"Why'd you do that?" Ephy asked.

"Do what?"

"Dump the coffee pot? I just made that, like, five minutes ago?"

"Oh!" It was so ingrained, I'd barely realized I'd done it. "For Mike." I nodded in his direction.

She made a vaguely scowling face that I took to mean she disapproved of me pouring out the coffee she'd just made—or that she understood what I was saying. It was hard to tell either way with her.

"Who am I looking for?" I asked.

"That guy."

I followed her outstretched finger across the room to a man studying one of the paintings on the wall. It was part of a new program I was testing out where local artists could display their work for customers to see and even buy at the end of the mini-exhibit. No one had said they wanted to purchase anything so far, but the seascapes had only been up for a day.

I grinned at the sight of the familiar figure. Since he was focused on the painting of a lobster boat heading out to sea at sunrise, I went ahead and grabbed a to-go cup, filled it to the brim with the piping-hot, freshly brewed coffee, snapped a lid on it, and made my way around the counter towards Mike. I handed him the cup wordlessly. He took it, nodded, and poured what must have been a quarter of it straight down his throat. I had no idea how he did it. If I tried doing that, my throat would be so scalded, I wouldn't be able to swallow for a week. But he did it several times a day. He must have built up a tolerance. Throat calluses or something.

As Mike headed for the door, I snuck up behind the man at the painting and wrapped my arms around his waist.

Chapter 4

MATT JUMPED SKY-HIGH. "WHO–WHA–?" He spun around with his hands up like he was getting ready to fight, but he exhaled as soon as his eyes landed on me. "Sheesh, Franny! You scared the crap out of me."

I giggled, even though everyone in the whole café had their eyes on us now. "I'm sorry. I didn't realize you were so engrossed in the painting."

His brow furrowed as his eyes moved around the café. "What painting?"

"The one you were looking at when I walked up?" When he still looked confused, I took his shoulders and turned him back around to face the painting.

He looked at it like he'd never seen it, even

though he'd been staring at it moments before. "Oh. That's cool. When did you get it?"

I sighed. "We put it up yesterday as part of the exhibition." I waved my hand around at all the other paintings of the beach and the ocean that adorned the walls.

"Oh, right. Sorry, I forgot about that." He raked his fingers through his thick, dark hair, making it adorably tousled.

Obviously, I needed to promote the art display more if my own boyfriend hadn't remembered, or even noticed the art hanging right in front of his face. "Everything okay?" I asked, noticing the worry line creasing the space between his eyebrows.

He exhaled slowly and ran his fingers through his hair again. "Yeah. Work's just been wearing me out lately. That McClusky project has been a nightmare."

He wasn't exaggerating. His latest project at work had been keeping him there into the wee hours for weeks now. I'd barely seen him for more than a couple hours at a time and only on the weekends—and we only lived two houses apart. Even when we had scraped out time to spend together, it had mostly been him dozing off on the couch while some sporting event I wasn't interested in played on the TV. I hadn't had the heart to wake him up or make him do anything more strenuous than moving a burger from the plate on his lap up to his mouth. Seeing him during daylight hours—on a weekday, no less!—felt positively luxurious at this point.

"So, to what do I owe the pleasure?" I snaked my arm back around his waist and snuggled myself into his chest.

He pulled me toward him and brushed his lips against the top of my head—more demonstrative than I, with my New England reserve, could usually stand in public, but I felt like I hadn't seen him in ages and couldn't get enough of his touch. "I thought I'd come by and see my girl. And pick up a gallon or so of coffee."

I looked up at him questioningly.

He gave me a tired smile. "They're having the quarterly birthday party at the office, and I couldn't get anything done, so I figured I'd work from home for the afternoon. I'll pass out the second my butt hits the couch if I don't have a barrel of caffeine to keep me going. You don't have any IV bags you could load up for me, do you?"

I laughed softly, even though it hurt my heart to hear him sound so exhausted. "No, but I can definitely load up a couple of boxes of coffee for you."

He nodded wearily and kissed the top of my head again. "That would be great, Franny. Thank you."

Reluctantly, I let him go and walked back around the counter to where Ephy stood looking at me with an expression that seemed to be a cross between disgust and bewilderment. "We need to make up a box of coffee," I said. "Do you know how to do that yet?"

She raised one pierced eyebrow, turned around to where the flattened boxes were stored, and pulled one out. I took that as a yes.

Sure enough, she quickly had the box assembled, filled, and sitting on the counter next to where Matt was leaning, looking dazed. "I take it this guy doesn't pay either?"

"Not today."

He actually did pay occasionally, mostly when he insisted on it. He'd remind me that I'd be out of business in a week if I fed everyone for free, which was an exaggeration but basically true. I still felt silly taking his money, though. It wasn't as though his free coffee alone would bankrupt the café. Just between Sammy and me, we drank as much free coffee in a day as he did in a week. But it wasn't worth arguing about, so I didn't. And, in any case, he was too lost in his thoughts today to think about it.

I grabbed the coffee box off the counter. "Did you drive over?"

Matt nodded as he tried to gently extract the box from my grasp. "Yeah, came straight from work. Give me that."

I pulled the box away. "No, I have it. I'll carry it out to the car for you."

"I think I can handle it, Franny."

"It's good customer service! Customer service is what keeps people coming in."

He looked down at me with one eyebrow raised and held his hand out.

"If I give it to you, I have no reason to walk you out to your car," I confessed, batting my eyes at him a little bit.

The corner of his lips twitched up. "You being my girlfriend who loves me isn't enough of a reason?"

I sighed and handed him the box. I never could resist that look.

"Ephy, I'm going to walk Matt out." I grabbed a bag and reached into the pastry case for a couple of cookies to send with Matt.

"Yeah, I caught that," she said in a monotone.

As soon as the door swung closed between us, Matt glanced over at me out of the corner of his eye. "Ephy, huh? Interesting name."

"She's an interesting girl."

Matt looked at me like he could tell there was more to the story. We'd seen each other so little lately that I'd only managed to tell him that I'd hired Ephy and nothing at all about how quirky she was.

"I'll tell you later," I muttered.

I noticed with dismay that Matt's car was parked on the street almost right outside the café. Normally, it wouldn't have mattered, but today it meant that all of the kisses I'd been hoping to steal would be in full view of all my customers. It wasn't exactly what I'd been hoping for when I followed him outside. I told myself I'd just have to wait until I closed up for the night and hope he wasn't still engrossed in work or so tired he'd already fallen asleep.

Matt popped open the passenger-side door and nestled the box of coffee on the floorboard for the nearly quarter-mile trip from the café to his house. He shut the door again.

"Well, I guess I'd better get back inside," I said.

I leaned in for a quick peck on the lips, but he stopped me.

"Actually, there's another reason why I stopped by."

"What's up?" I tried to sound casual, but something in his expression had me on edge.

He leaned back against the car and sighed. "I feel really bad about this."

Now I was really worried.

He stared at the ground and ran his fingers through his hair. Finally, he looked up. "I dropped the ball. I totally forgot that your birthday's coming up. I wanted to do something really special for you, but then this project came up, and I've been so busy I haven't even done laundry in three weeks, let alone planned something for your birthday. I—I can't even think of anything you've said you want. I was thinking a necklace or some earrings or something, but you don't wear very much jewelry. And then I thought maybe a sweater, but that wouldn't be a good gift, would it?"

I shook my head. "Not this time of year, no."

Matt sighed. "I know this is terrible, but could you just tell me something you want and I'll get it for you? And if I can get it online, that's even better because I don't know when I'm going to make it to the store."

"Aw, Matty!" I leaned in and gave him a hug. "Don't worry about it. It's totally not a big deal." He started to protest, but I stopped him. "All I want is to get to spend some actual time with you. We can go out to dinner somewhere nice, maybe Osteria di Monica, just enjoy each other's company."

He relaxed a little, but still looked uneasy. "I want to get you something, though. You deserve to have a present on your birthday—more than one!"

"But I don't *need* presents. All I need is you." I looked up and saw the expression on his face. He wasn't going to be happy with just taking me out for a nice meal. "But if you really feel that strongly about it, look at the *USA Today* bestsellers list and get me whatever book looks interesting. I'll read it and love it and always remember that you got it for me."

He looked doubtful but nodded slowly. I could tell that he was too exhausted and distracted by work to argue anymore. We exchanged goodbyes, and I herded him into the car to head home. I secretly hoped he would fall asleep on the couch before he even got his laptop open, but I suspected he would actually start chugging the coffee as soon as he walked in the door and be wired well into the night.

I watched him drive away and then went back inside. "I'll be in the back," I told Ephy as I passed her. I closed the office door behind me and sat down at the desk with my head in my hands. I was worried about Matt, yes, especially since he skipped out on the office birthday party, but there was something else—something worse.

Matt had been worried that he didn't have a present yet for my birthday, which would come up in three weeks, but his birthday was even sooner than that, and it hadn't even crossed my mind until that moment.

Chapter 5

I SPENT most of that evening curled up on Matt's couch, trying to think of what to do for him for his birthday while he furiously worked away, barely even acknowledging my presence. Latte, my beloved Berger Picard rescue dog, lay curled up against my leg, nudging my hand insistently whenever I failed to keep with his petting needs. I otherwise amused myself with a marathon of a reality show featuring a gaggle of glammed-up, look-alike sisters constantly bickering with each other over who borrowed whose dress or something else equally insignificant. In one episode, they planned a birthday party for one of their interchangeable boyfriends, but I didn't think I could afford a private jet to fly us to Mexico for an alcohol-soaked party with one hundred of Matt's nearest and dearest. I didn't even think Matt had one hundred people who would qualify as his nearest and dearest.

That episode did give me one great idea, though. Jetting off to Mexico might have been a no-go, but that didn't mean I couldn't throw him a party. I loved throwing parties! They were a prime excuse for baking. Not that I needed one, but a party did give me a reason to make something a little fancier and more time-consuming than the standard fare we served in the café.

I nudged him. He didn't move. I nudged him again. Without looking up, he held up one finger. I leaned over so I could see his screen. It was some kind of diagram with rainbow-hued lines zigzagging across it. Matt used his cursor to grab onto one of the orange lines and drag it the tiniest bit to the side. He changed views, changed it back, and nudged the line over a tiny bit more.

"Okay, what's up?"

"There's something I've been thinking about, and I wanted to run it by you." I conveniently left out that I'd been thinking about it for the past five minutes, not five weeks. "What do you think about throwing a big party for your birthday?"

He stared at me for so long that I started to wonder if he hadn't heard me. Then, very slowly, he said, "A party?"

I nodded, shifting my position on the couch so I was facing him more. Latte army-crawled his way back onto the prime position he preferred on my lap. I stroked his head with one hand and put the other on Matt's shoulder. "Yes! It would be so much fun! We'd invite your friends over, I could make all the food, we could put a football game on—"

"It's May, Franny."

"I know! Your birthday is in May!"

"There's no football in May."

I waved him off. "Oh, well, whatever. We can put something you like on. Just think how much fun it will be!"

He looked skeptical. "It would just be four or five guys, Franny."

I mentally counted up the number of guys he hung out with, and four or five might have been a little high. "Well, not when you invite their wives and girlfriends too. And we could invite some of my friends and people we know in town to round things out. It would actually be really fun!" I was set on this idea now. Completely committed. All I needed was for Matt to agree. "So what do you think?"

"I think it sounds more like a Fran party than a Matt party."

"Except that it's for *your* birthday."

He looked at me, and I saw the corners of his eyes beginning to crinkle in the way that made me feel like a sixteen-year-old with her first boyfriend again. "How about we make it a combined party for both our birthdays?"

I wanted to protest, to argue that this was something I wanted to do for him, not for myself. I didn't need a party. I didn't need to have a gathering of all the people I knew and loved, who'd made my time back in Cape Bay so wonderful. I'd been down and broken when I arrived, and yet my friends—new and old—had made it a better experience than I could have ever imagined. I didn't need that. But who was I kidding? I definitely wanted it. "Are you sure? I meant this to be something special for you, not a party for me."

He smiled tenderly and brushed my hair back from my face. "Nothing makes me happier than seeing you happy."

I studied his face, trying to figure out whether he really meant it or if he was just trying to get me to leave him alone so he could get back to work. At the same time, I fought with myself over whether it was wrong to give in to the idea of a joint party. Finally, I gave in and threw my arms around his neck. "It'll be great, I promise."

"I know it will." He patted my arm and kissed my cheek. "And I know you're going to be very excited about planning it, but I need to get back to my plans here now, so if you need my input, we'll have to talk about it later. But I'm sure that whatever you want to do will be great. Especially if you're catering." He grinned at me for a second then gestured at his computer. And as quick as that, I'd lost him to his work again. This time, though, I didn't mind too much because I had a party to plan.

I pulled out my phone to find a good date on my calendar. There was a weekend between our birthdays that would be perfect. I immediately sent Matt a calendar event so he would have that time blocked off. Now that I felt like the pressure was off, I quickly decided I'd get him tickets to see the Patriots... or Red Sox... or Bruins... or whoever had a game coming up I could get tickets to. We could go up to Boston and make a whole night—or even weekend!—out of it.

With that settled, I started thinking about all the delicious things I could make for the party. There would have to be cake, of course—it wouldn't be a birthday party without cake. Two cakes, since there were two of us. His would be chocolate and peanut butter—or maybe caramel. I'd do something seasonal and fruity for mine. Maybe a play on a strawberry-rhubarb pie. That would be delicious. And, of course, there would be appetizers—bacon-wrapped asparagus, some homemade Italian meatballs, maybe lobster bites. Punch, of course. I had a great recipe that had been passed down from my mom and was always fruity and bubbly and delicious. We'd have some non-alcoholic for the kids, but we could spike another bowl for the grown-ups.

And desserts! I could make so many desserts. Maybe I could even enlist Sammy and the girls at the café to help me out so we could have more options. I'd have cookies and miniature pies and tarts. And I could use puff pastry shells for the tarts. I loved puff pastry! I hardly ever made it because of how labor-intensive it was, but for a double birthday celebration, it would be perfect. And with the party date I'd chosen still over a week out, I'd have plenty of time to make as much as I thought I could possibly need.

I started jotting down in my phone all the different things I could possibly make with puff pastry. Aside from tarts, I could make cream horns and mille-feuille and pigs in blankets and brie en croute. And those were just to start. Aside from the buttery, flaky deliciousness of the pastry, my favorite thing about it was how versatile it was. I could make a million different things with it, either sweet or savory. And they'd all have that perfect, delicious crust.

The more I thought about it, the more excited I got. Not just about the food, although I found that pretty exciting, but also about the prospect of gathering all our friends together and celebrating. I started mentally running through who I'd want to invite. Sammy and everyone from the café of course, as well as their significant others and families. I'd even invite Ephy. I barely knew her, but I didn't want her to feel left out. Especially not when the more I thought about it, the more people I wanted to invite. Matt may have only had a few guys he hung out with on a regular basis, but I knew there were many more people that he was friendly with who he'd enjoy having there.

I stopped to take a look at the list of people I'd added to my phone. It was getting long. I looked around Matt's house. It wasn't big, and mine wasn't any bigger. They were both built in the post-war suburban housing explosion and were simple mirror-image Cape Cod-style bungalows. We could have the party there, but I'd have to cut the guest list dramatically.

I sighed. Half the fun of the party would be having everyone there. The only way to invite everyone would be to rent someplace out, and Cape Bay wasn't big enough to have a lot of party venues available, especially not when I'd want it to have a full kitchen so I could do my final prep there. Maybe I could charm one of the local restaurants into letting us have it there and allowing me to use the kitchen. Maybe Fiesta Mexicana? Or—

Matt glanced at me out of the corner of his eye as I smacked my forehead.

"Never mind," I muttered, waving him off. I couldn't believe I'd overlooked the most perfect, most obvious solution. We'd have the party at the café.

Chapter 6

BY THE TIME the day of the party arrived, an aching sensation had become my feet's default state. Aside from the hours I worked in the café, I'd stayed late every night, working on the food for the party. I'd prepared everything I could beforehand and finished almost everything earlier that day. A few things would still have to be popped in the oven closer to party time, but everything else was done except for the punch and one last batch of puff pastry mini-tartlets I'd decided to make at the last minute. Unfortunately, I'd already gone through all the puff pastry I'd prepared, so I had to prep another batch. I'd considered whether I really wanted to go to all that trouble, but ever since the idea of lemon tartlets had crossed my mind, my mouth had been watering in anticipation of them.

I had the basic dough prepped and chilled, but that was the easy part. I got a one-pound slab of butter out of the freezer—freezing the butter made it so much easier to make puff pastry—and took it over to the granite countertop, where I had a sheet tray loaded with ice sitting. It was a trick my grandmother had taught me years and years ago—chill the countertop where you'd be working, and you'd buy yourself a little extra time with your dough before it needed to go back in the fridge.

I slid the baking sheet aside and layered the hunk of butter between a couple sheets of plastic wrap. Then, I grabbed my rolling pin and went to town, beating the two-inch by four-inch butter into a flat, six-by-six square.

"What's going on?" Sammy asked, looking concerned as she came into the kitchen.

"What?" I paused my butter-beating so I could hear her.

"What are you doing? It sounds like you're trying to break down a wall or something."

"Oh! Sorry!" I held up the rolling pin and gestured at the butter before I realized that I'd made all the puff pastry after hours, and Sammy had never been there to witness the process. She'd tasted some of the finished product, but she hadn't seen how all those buttery, flaky layers came about. "I have to pound out the butter to make the next batch of puff pastry."

She looked skeptical, raising her eyebrows. "Will it take much longer? The customers look kind of concerned."

I grimaced. I had been so set on making more puff pastry, I hadn't really thought about how loud it would be out in the café. I looked down at the butter. It was getting close, but it still needed to be beaten a little thinner. I looked at Sammy. "Maybe another thirty seconds? Or a minute?" It didn't sound like much time, but I knew it would probably seem like an eternity to the people sitting in the café, who were just trying to enjoy a nice cup of coffee and maybe a pastry. "I'll get it done as fast as I can. Apologize to them for me. And make sure they all know about the party tonight."

Once I'd come around to the idea of having the party at the café and discussed it with Matt, we both realized that we might as well make it into an open house instead of trying to pick out who we'd invite. We knew and loved almost everyone in town, so why not invite them all? We'd probably be inviting more people than not anyway. I'd had a sign up in the café for almost a week, and I'd made sure to tell the girls to mention it to anyone who came in. The more the merrier, after all. And it wasn't about gifts either. We'd decided there wasn't anything we needed or wanted, and we'd be much happier if the money people would have spent on a gift went to something more meaningful. The signs I'd put up around town clearly stated, "No Gifts, Please, but Donations to the Cape Bay Animal Shelter will be happily accepted at the door." It was my way of including Latte in our celebration, since I couldn't have him at the actual party—the health department wouldn't have allowed it. Other than dogs, though, everyone in town was invited, and I hoped that Sammy reminding customers of that would go at least a little way in helping them to overlook the banging. The promise of pastry tended to do that for people.

Sammy nodded and left, closing the door tightly behind her for what little sound protection it would provide. It wasn't meant for that, and I seriously doubted it would do any good, but I understood her point. Trying to be quieter wouldn't do any good— frozen butter took a heavy hand to flatten. Besides, the last thing I wanted to do was to give the butter a chance to melt before I got it to the right size. Melted butter was death to puff pastry. All I could do was try to do it faster, so that was what I did.

When I finally got it thin enough, I grabbed the dough out of the refrigerator and laid it on the counter with the butter on top, covering the bottom two-thirds of the dough I'd already rolled out and shaped. I did a letter fold on it, bringing the unbuttered top section down over the butter then folding the bottom buttered part up on top. Now I had two layers of butter in between three layers of dough.

A good start, but two butter layers were nowhere near enough to get the delicate, flaky crust I was going for. I rotated the dough ninety degrees, rolled it back out to its original size, then did the letter fold again—top third down, bottom third up. By my estimation, that was six layers, but I still wanted more. I wrapped the dough up in plastic wrap and popped it back in the fridge to keep the butter layers nice and cold. It would need to be in there for twenty or thirty minutes before I took it back out and did two more letter folds. Then it would go back in the fridge for one more round. By the end, the dough would have nearly a thousand layers of butter that, when baked, would puff up the dough and create the flakiness I was looking for.

With plenty of time before I needed to work on the puff pastry again, I decided to get a head start on the punch. It was easy enough that it could be mixed right before party time, but I wanted to go ahead and freeze some for ice cubes. Nothing ruined a good bowl of punch like a bunch of melted ice cubes watering it down. I got everything I needed out of the refrigerator—some raspberry sorbet, pineapple, and a bottle of lemon-lime soda. Simple but delicious. Although it was counterintuitive, I had pre-thawed my frozen punch ingredients. In my opinion, it made the punch so much easier to mix evenly without odd pockets of different flavors as the frozen ingredients slowly melted.

I poured everything together into a large punch bowl and mixed it together thoroughly. Then I grabbed a ladle and poured some into a cup. It was so delicious. Fruity from the raspberries in the sorbet and light and bubbly from the soda. I'd add a dose of rum to one of the punch bowls at the party, but truth be told, it didn't need it. It was every bit as good without alcohol as with it. I helped myself to another cup before making myself get back to work. I would have plenty of time to drink punch at the party.

I filled up every ice tray I'd been able to find between my house, Matt's, and the café. I even had a couple that Sammy had brought in for us to use. We had a big ice machine that provided all the ice we usually used in the café, but that was hooked into the water line, just like our espresso machines were, and I didn't think it was a good idea to try to pour punch into it. If I was lucky, we would have just had fruity ice for a while. If I was unlucky, the whole machine would probably get gummed from the sugar in the punch, and I'd have to buy a new one. It was easier to just use the few that I'd managed to scrounge up.

I covered the punch with plastic wrap and wedged it back into the fridge alongside the containers of sorbet, pineapple juice, and soda that I had ready and waiting to use for more punch. Both of our industrial-size fridges were completely packed with food for the party that night. I had no idea how many people would attend—a downside of making it an open-house event—or how much they would eat, so I might have gone a little over-board on the food prep. I just wanted to make sure everyone was well fed! I would have felt like a terrible hostess if anyone went away hungry.

I did the next fold-and-turn on the puff pastry

then popped it back in the fridge. I needed to get the lemon curd tart filling going. Fortunately, it was a pretty straightforward recipe that I'd made a million times. As long as I didn't scramble the eggs, I'd be fine.

I zested a bunch of lemons then poured in the sugar and mixed them up. Then I dropped in the eggs and some lemon juice, put the whole thing in a pan on the stove, and cooked the mixture for a few minutes. Then I added a pinch of salt and some butter, strained it all, and left it to cool. And I pulled it all off with no major disasters. As soon as I got the puff pastry done and cooked, I'd be ready to go.

Or so I thought until I caught a glimpse of myself in the mirror next to the door and realized I'd have to find time to go home and get a shower if I didn't want to show up at my own party with flour in my hair and specks of lemon curd all over my face.

Chapter 7

I MANAGED to get the café cleaned, rearranged, and decorated, the food all prepared, and myself cleaned up in time for the party to start. All that was thanks in no small part to Sammy, who I felt like was sharing my brain and providing two extra hands for me. Every time I turned to ask her to help me with something, I found her already doing it, whether it was carrying food out to the tables or adjusting a decoration or putting out a sign-in sheet so Matt and I could thank everyone personally for coming in the days after the party.

Well, who was I kidding? Matt would thank his buddies for showing up that night and then never think of it again. That was probably a fair approach to take, but if a lot of people showed up—which I

53

hoped they did, for the sake of the animal shelter, but also because I had made quite a lot of food—it might be hard to get around and say hello to everyone during the party. With a list, I could go thank them afterward.

Matt managed to pull himself away from his work and showed up early, like I'd asked. I was thrilled because Sammy and I needed help moving a few tables around to create more space for people to mingle.

"Oh good!" I exclaimed as he walked in. "Could you get that four-top from the back and bring it over next to this other one?"

"Hi, honey, I missed you too." He sauntered over and looked down at me with a wry smile.

"Sorry, I'm just trying to get everything all set so we're not still working on it when people start arriving." I gave him a quick peck on the lips before going back to the napkins I was arranging in a fan pattern on the table.

"Relax." He glanced down at his watch. "The party doesn't start for twenty minutes."

My head snapped up to look at the large cast-iron clock that hung on one of the café's exposed brick walls. "Twenty minutes? Forget these napkins! We need to get plates and forks and cups and—"

Matt put his hands on my shoulders. "Calm down, Franny. We're going to get it all done. Just take a deep breath. It'll be okay."

I looked at him like I thought he was crazy—because I did. I was sure there was no way to get everything done and make everything perfect in twenty minutes. And that was assuming no one showed up until the official start time. Someone always did. No one else would show up for another half hour or so, but there was always that one person who was there before they were supposed to be. Whoever it was, I wanted to be sure we were ready when they walked in.

Fortunately, the first people to trickle in were more like family than guests—the people we would have invited even if we were just having a small gathering at the house. Sammy's boyfriend, Ryan, was the first to come in, followed shortly by Rhonda—who also worked for me—and her husband, then my high-schoolers, Becky and Amanda, with their families. There was no sign of Ephy as the official seven o'clock start time came and went, but I reminded myself that she was joining us to celebrate, not coming in to work. She could be as late as she wanted, and it would be fine. Besides, other people were starting to filter in.

Some friends, some acquaintances, some people who I didn't really know but recognized from the café.

Almost everyone signed the sheet of paper serving as a guest book, and I saw lots of people slipping money into the collections box for the animal shelter. I wondered briefly if it had been a bad idea to leave it so close to the door—it would be so easy for someone to grab it and run out—but I reassured myself that we were in Cape Bay, which wasn't exactly a hotbed of crime. Well, for the most part. We *had* had more than our share of murders in town lately, but it was a safe town otherwise, with just some vandalism and the occasional petty theft taking up most of the police department's time.

I gradually started to relax and enjoy the party. People were milling around, chatting with each other, eating the snacks I'd spent so much time preparing, and generally having fun.

"Happy birthday, Francesca. It's a lovely party."

I turned around to see Mary Ellen, who ran the gift shop across the street, smiling broadly at me. She looked as polished and refined as ever, with her blond hair perfectly coiffed and a cobalt-blue jumpsuit topped with jewelry I was sure came from one of the local artists whose work she stocked in her shop. I only hoped I looked as good as her when I was her age.

"Mary Ellen! Thank you for coming." I held out my arm and gave her a big hug. "Have you had anything to eat yet?"

"I've been nibbling my way through. Those canapés with the Italian sausage are divine."

I thanked her and glanced over at the tables holding all the food to make sure they were still well stocked.

Mary Ellen touched my arm and leaned in. "As a woman who has thrown her share of parties, let me give you a little tip. Stop worrying so much and enjoy the party. The more fun you have, the more fun your guests will have." She smiled warmly at me. Then her smile broadened as she looked over my shoulder at someone across the room. I looked over and spotted a dapper-looking older gentleman making eyes at her.

"Who's that?" I knew I'd seen him in the café before, but I hadn't met him yet.

"He's new in town. Just retired here after a long career in law up in Boston. Handsome, don't you think?"

He was rather handsome in that old-enough-to-be-my-father kind of way. I'd never really known my father—he and my mother had broken up when I was too small to still have any memory of him— but the man across the café was about the age he would be now. I guessed. I didn't even know that much about him.

But I didn't want to think about it right now, so I put it out of my head and focused back on Mary Ellen. She, however, was still looking across at the man with a coy smile on her face. She batted her eyes, glanced away, and then looked back. She could have taught a master class in flirting with the way she was acting. She tucked a strand of her blond hair behind her ear. It was impressive, really. If I were looking for tips, she'd be the person I'd talk to. It wasn't just for show, either—Mary Ellen was perpetually popular with the retirement-aged men in Cape Bay.

Mary Ellen's new beau was making his way toward us now, a cup of punch in each hand. Mary Ellen touched my arm again. "If you'll excuse me." She started toward him then stopped and lowered her voice to a whisper. "Don't forget to relax." Then she flashed the man a brilliant smile and walked over to him.

She was right. The party was supposed to be fun, not stressful. I needed to relax and enjoy myself. I headed for the table with the punch, stopping along the way to greet friends and neighbors and thank them all for coming.

I caught Sammy's eye and mouthed "thank you" as she refilled the punch bowls.

"Hey, Fran!"

I looked up to see the brilliant blue eyes of Todd Caruthers smiling down at me. "Todd! Hi!"

He wrapped his arms around me and pulled me against the hard muscles of his chest. Todd and I had gone to high school together. Back then, he'd been the too-attractive-for-his-own-good, all-American star athlete. To be honest, not much had changed since then. He'd gotten older, yes, but he was still distractingly handsome and just as in shape as ever—maybe even more. It made sense, given that he owned the cleverly named Todd's Gym out on the edge of town near the marina.

"How are you doing, Todd?"

"Good! Good." He ran his fingers through his surfer-blond hair. "You know, business slowed down after the thing with Joe, but it's starting to pick up again. I'm hoping to get some more traffic by offering day passes to the tourists. Get the ladies who don't want to miss their yoga class, you know?"

I nodded. "The thing with Joe" he'd referred to

was actually a murder that had happened in the gym's parking lot. I hadn't realized business had slowed down for him after that, but it made sense. Even though the murder had been solved, I could see someone being put off from the place. It wasn't fair, but people didn't usually consider fairness when they were thinking about their safety.

We chatted for a few more minutes before I resumed my mission to get to the refreshments table. I was feeling more than a little parched. A cup of rum-spiked punch was just the thing I needed to quench my thirst and help me relax a little. I grabbed one of the Italian sausage canapés and popped it into my mouth on my way to the punch bowl. Ephy was standing near it, leaning against the wall, holding a cup of water. "Don't like the punch?" I asked.

As usual, she shrugged. "I don't like, like, sweet stuff."

I wondered if that explained her personality. "Have you gotten anything to eat? There's a lot that isn't sweet."

She shrugged again. I decided it wasn't worth the effort to try to make pleasant conversation with her when I was supposed to be kicking back and having fun. Instead, I just ladled myself some punch.

"Does that have alcohol?" someone beside me asked.

I turned and saw Melissa, one of Sammy's friends. I'd gotten to know her while investigating the murder at Todd's Gym the year before. Her ex had been killed, and even though they were broken up, she had been devastated. She had somehow managed to keep it together for their little girl. As it always did, the sight of her dark curls, blue eyes, and cheerful face made me smile. And then my smile broadened as I glanced down and realized she'd grown a little since the last time I saw her. I caught my breath and blurted out "What's this?" before realizing how terrible it would be if she wasn't actually six or so months pregnant like I thought.

Fortunately, she grinned and turned to the side, putting her hands on the top and bottom of her belly to emphasize its size. "I'm having another baby!" she squealed.

"Congratulations!" I gave her a hug, taking care not to splash any of the red punch on her white blouse. "Boy or girl?"

"Another little girl!"

I asked her a few more questions like when she was due and how she was feeling. Then I remembered what had started our conversation. "This bowl has alcohol. That one down there doesn't."

She gave me a brilliant smile. "Thank you! And happy birthday!"

As she walked away, I finally took a sip of my punch. My forehead wrinkled. Something about it didn't taste quite right. Not bad, necessarily, just not quite what it was like when I first made it. It was probably the Italian sausage I'd just eaten messing with my taste buds. The punch was still good, just different, and I drained my cup and refilled it then drained that and refilled it again.

I spotted Matt sitting at a table across the room and made my way over to him. As much as I enjoyed chatting with everyone who had turned out to help us celebrate, the party was for Matt and me, and I wanted to spend at least a little bit of time with him.

"Hey, gorgeous," he said as I walked up and took the seat next to him. "Good party. Everyone seems to be having a great time."

I surveyed the room, looking at all the small clusters of people chatting happily as they ate their hors d'oeuvres and sipped their punch.

I smiled up at Matt. "It's exactly what I wanted."

He smiled back, but the warmth that was usually in his eyes was missing. I looked at him a little more closely. His face was a little red, and his breathing seemed heavier than usual.

"Are you okay?"

He nodded. "Just not feeling great." He pulled at his T-shirt collar. "Is it warm in here?"

"A little." I felt his forehead. It was a little warm but also clammy. "Do you need to go lie down?"

He shook his head. "I'll be okay. Just don't be mad at me if I'm not moving around and talking to people too much."

I put my head on his shoulder. "I would never."

He shifted in his chair and pulled at his collar again.

"Do you want me to get you something to drink? Some more punch? Or water?"

"Some water might be good." His breathing sounded more labored already.

I got up and started making my way through the crowd over to the sink for some water. I hadn't made it very far when Mary Ellen's gentleman friend rushed past me on his way to the bathroom, clutching his hand over his mouth. As my eyes followed him, I saw Rhonda coming out of the other bathroom, looking decidedly green.

I stopped and looked around the room. More than a few people around the room were looking a little red-faced and sweaty like Matt. Some of the others just looked weak and pale. Worry started to flare up in my gut when something else flared up as well.

I barely made it to the bathroom to crouch in front of the toilet before my stomach clenched and everything I'd eaten that day came roaring back up.

Chapter 8

THE NEXT MORNING, I found myself huddled on
Matt's couch, wrapped in a blanket, willing myself
to feel less awful. I'd spent the night at Matt's place
because it was marginally closer to the café than my
own house two doors down was. With how terrible
I'd felt when I'd stumbled home the night before, I
didn't actually know if I would have made it the last
one hundred feet to my door. When Matt and I left
the café, I was feeling weak and shaky, but I could
walk, which was more than I could say for some of
the other people who'd come to the party.

By the time I'd stumbled out of the bathroom
the night before, after ignoring more than one
knock on the bathroom door, the café had been lit
up with the flashing red lights of the two ambu-

lances parked outside. I already felt terrible from the nausea that had sent me running to the bathroom, but the sight of them made me feel even worse. In all the time I'd spent planning the party, it had never occurred to me that it might end with paramedics making their way around the room, checking my guests' vital signs. Most people were sent home with instructions to rest, drink lots of fluids, and call 911 if they felt any worse, but several of them got hooked up to oxygen, loaded into the ambulance, and carted off to the hospital.

The worst part was that I had a sinking feeling that it was my fault.

During the few moments I'd had during the night when I didn't feel too sick to even think, I'd wracked my brain trying to think of somewhere that I might have cut a corner in my food prep or been sloppy with my cleaning or refrigeration. As hard as I tried, I couldn't think of anything. I'd prepared a lot of food and had to juggle multiple recipes and ingredients at a time, but I couldn't think of a single thing I might have done that could have caused cross-contamination or compromised the safety of the food. But I must have. All those people didn't get sick from nothing.

Matt was on the couch next to me, also in his

pajamas with a blanket wrapped around him. He'd been drifting in and out of sleep in between trips to the bathroom all night and looked, at the moment, closer to sleep than wakefulness. An occasional groan was the most coherent sound I'd heard from him in hours.

Latte lay curled up quietly between us, seemingly understanding that neither of one of us felt well enough to walk or play with him as usual. The poor little guy would have to make do with us occasionally shuffling to the back door to let him run outside for a minute.

In the easy chair off to the side of the couch, Detective Mike Stanton sat hunched over with a cup of coffee cradled in his hands. He seemed to be holding it and staring at it more than drinking it, an indication, I suspected, that he didn't actually feel much better than either of us did, even though he was up and dressed and out of his house.

He stared at the coffee cup for a few more seconds then put it down on the end table next to him and slowly drew a notebook and pen out of the pocket of his navy cargo pants. The detective flipped his notebook open and turned his bleary eyes toward me. "Any idea what happened, Fran?"

I started to shake my head but stopped as pain

shot through my skull and the nausea kicked up again. I could hardly move without feeling like I was going to be sick again, although my stomach had long since rid itself of all its contents. "No," I forced out.

"Not even a guess?" Even sick, Mike was a dogged investigator.

"Not really." I tried to move my lips and nothing else. "I figure it must be food poisoning. I've been trying to think of whether I accidentally left something out too long or didn't cool it fast enough, but I don't think I did. I can't imagine what happened unless maybe something came in contaminated."

Mike nodded and scribbled something down on his notepad. "Where do you get your supplies?"

"Coffee I get from a distributor, mostly, but there are a couple of farms I order from direct—"

"The stuff you made last night."

"Milk, butter, and eggs come from local farms. The Italian sausage came from a local farm. Flour and that kind of thing comes from a distributor. I got some stuff at the grocery store." I was exhausted from just that little bit of talking.

Mike bobbed his head in what I took for a nod.

"I'll need a list of everyone you bought things from for last night."

Did that mean he thought something had been contaminated before it got to me? And was that a matter for the police? As much of a relief as it would be to find out that it wasn't my fault, it didn't make up for all those people getting so sick by a long shot.

The detective leaned back in his chair, cringing as he did. He took a couple of breaths with his eyes squeezed closed. He opened them again, blinked a few times and tried to focus on my face. "They ran tests at the hospital on the people who were brought in."

"Was it salmonella?" That was the first type of food poisoning that came to mind. And with the number of eggs I'd used, it would make sense if they were contaminated before I got them.

Mike inclined his head slightly.

"*E. coli*?"

His eye twitched like he would have raised his eyebrow if his head didn't hurt so much.

"Trichinosis?"

"Did you clean everything up before you left last night?"

"No." If I'd been feeling better, I would have

been ashamed of myself for leaving the café a mess and all that food out to spoil. Of course, if the food had made everyone sick, there was no use saving it anyway, but it was still embarrassing to have left the café such a mess when anyone could walk by, look in the windows, and see what a disaster everything was. I was almost too sick to care about that, though. Almost.

"Sammy clean it up this morning?"

"No," I croaked. "She's sick too. And Rhonda. The girls are too young. And Ephy—" I stopped. I'd called Sammy and Rhonda earlier that morning to see how they were feeling, but they both felt like death warmed over. With all three of us sick, there was no point in opening the café, so I'd called the girls and then Ephy to let them know we would be closed. The girls had been feeling fine, but they were both picky eaters and left early besides, so it didn't strike me as particularly strange. But Ephy felt fine, too, and even sounded almost perky. Perky for Ephy anyway. When I'd expressed my surprise, she'd volunteered that she must not have eaten whatever made everyone sick. But that wasn't really any different than the girls not being sick, was it? "Ephy's too new to be there by herself. We're closed until we all get back on our feet."

Mike grunted and wrote something down on his notepad. He stared down at it for a moment before turning back to me. He spent a long time looking at me, so long that I started to feel uncomfortable and shifted a little on the couch. "It wasn't food poisoning."

I stared back at him, trying to process what could have made all of us so sick if it wasn't food poisoning.

"They were poisoned."

If my abdomen hadn't already ached from spending all night huddled over a toilet, I would have felt like someone punched me in the gut. "Poisoned? With real, actual poison? What? Why? Who would do something like that?"

This time, he did raise an eyebrow while looking me dead in the eye.

I waited for him to explain until my nausea seemed to fade away as realization slowly dawned for me. "You—you can't—you don't—Mike, you know me—" I searched his face for some sign that he wasn't serious. It was cruel to joke about something like that, and I'd never known Mike to be cruel, but maybe the sickness was messing with his sense of decency.

He looked at me with expressionless eyes. "Fran,

I'm going to need your permission to search your house and the café."

Tears sprang to my eyes. I still had some fragile hope that he was joking.

A flicker of regret passed across his eyes. His voice was softer. "Otherwise, I'm going to get a search warrant."

Chapter 9

AS SOON AS I agreed to let them search my house and the café, he sent me to get dressed. Then he loaded me into his squad car and drove me over to the café. He must have had the crime scene team on standby because they were already parked outside when we pulled up.

One of the crime scene techs had to unlock the door for me because my hands were shaking too much to get my key into the lock. He pulled the door open and held it for me to walk in first.

The café was exactly like we'd left it before. The tables loaded down with food, big bowls of punch at either end still half full, discarded paper plates and plastic cups scattered on every available surface, some with food still on them. Some of the food even had bites taken out of it. It was the kind of thing you would see at a disaster site where everyone had fled unexpectedly and in a hurry, leaving the remnants of the last normal moments behind. If you dropped a group of people into the room, they could pick back up exactly where they left off, and no one would know the difference.

I would, though.

The night before, the tantalizing smell of fresh-baked pastries, both sweet and savory, had filled the café. The rich, buttery aroma of freshly made cookies and puff pastry, the hint of citrus from the lemon tarts, the warm spices of the sausage—they'd all blended together in an enticing mix that beckoned our guests inside and welcomed them to our party.

Now, it smelled stale—stale food, stale air, and stale—well, a lot of people had been very nauseated, and the bathrooms hadn't been cleaned. The scene was far more repellant than inviting. And the scattered detritus of the party just drove it home. The night didn't end because people were ready to go—it ended because they were too sick to stay.

"All right, guys." Mike's voice boomed behind me as he and the crime scene techs started filling the café. "We believe the poison was ingested, so we

want samples of all the food on the table and—"
He stopped and looked around. "You may as well
get the stuff people left on the tables too."

The techs swarmed the room, fanning out with
plastic evidence bags in hand, ready to be filled with
the food I'd made—food the police thought had
been poisoned. Even though I knew the food was
inedible, my gut reaction was still that it was such a
waste of food.

"Do you want us to take all of it, Detective?"
one of the techs asked, his hand poised over a plat-
ter, ready to slide every last slice of the mille-feuille
into his bag.

Mike studied the table for a few seconds then
shook his head. "Just grab a few of each. If the tests
come back inconclusive, we'll come back for more."

I realized then that the café wasn't getting
cleaned up anytime soon.

The tech dropped a couple slices of the mille-
feuille into the bag and moved over to the fudgey
chocolate chip cookies next to them. Mike stopped
him as he reached out for them. "One thing per
bag." He rolled his eyes and looked at me for
sympathy. As much as I wanted to offer it, I couldn't
quite muster it under the circumstances.

He seemed to understand, shoving his hands

in his pockets and turning back to survey the techs. After a moment, he glanced back my way. "You can sit down if you want. Probably be a while."

I sank down into the closest chair. The techs were everywhere, like a colony of ants moving in on a picnic. I watched them warily. I'd seen enough TV shows where the aftermath of a search looked about the same as a thorough burglary—drawers emptied, shelves cleared, everything everywhere. I hoped the local guys would be more considerate than that. Of course, they were from the county, so they didn't actually know me like the Cape Bay officers did.

"Let's be careful, guys. We don't need to toss the place," Mike said, giving a hard look at a tech behind the counter who was being a little haphazard with the glass jars I used to display different varieties and roasts of beans. I liked having them to show customers when they had questions. Being able to hand someone a few beans to sniff and roll around in their hand went a long way towards helping them understand what differentiated one from another. Plus, they looked pretty and made good décor.

"Sorry about that," Mike muttered in my direction. "I'm trying to keep them in line." He looked over at me with something like regret.

I nodded slightly—as much as I could without sending another wave of pain through my skull—and put my elbow on the table next to me. The sign-in sheet and donation box from the night before were still sitting on it. One of us should have locked that up before we left the night before. Someone could have stolen it easily. I'd been too sick to think even of that the night before.

I pulled the box toward me and checked under the lid. I didn't know how much money had been in it the night before, but there was still a pile of bills and checks inside, so I didn't think anyone had tampered with it. I'd have to ask Mike about locking it up or going ahead and taking it over to the animal shelter. I didn't know what I'd do if the crime scene techs wanted to take it for some test or other. Find out how much it was and go ahead and write a check, I guessed. I hated the thought of the animal shelter missing out because of what happened last night.

I pushed the box away and pulled over the sign-in sheet. Well, it wasn't so much a sign-in sheet as a sort of guest book. A guest sheet, really, since it was only one piece of paper. Names filled one side completely and went two-thirds of the way down the other side. We'd had a good turnout. It was a shame how the night ended up.

I scanned down the list, idly looking for any names that stood out. Names I didn't recognize were scattered in amongst the many I did. It didn't mean I didn't know them—there were lots of people I ran into around town who I recognized and would chat with but whose names I didn't actually know. And there were plenty more who I only knew by first name. Still, I recognized many of the names. Todd Caruthers, Mary Ellen Chapman, Karli, who worked the front desk at the gym, Sammy, Melissa, Rhonda and her husband, Sammy's friend Dawn, Dean Howard from Howard Jewelers. So many people I knew and loved. I'd just wanted to celebrate with them, and I'd ended up sending some of them to the hospital.

Well, not *me*. I hadn't actually done anything to put them in the hospital. But someone had. Someone had come into my café and poisoned the food I had prepared for our big birthday celebration. I felt violated. I felt angry. I felt offended. And I felt helpless. I didn't know who could have done such a thing.

The girls who worked with me in the café had

the most access, but I couldn't imagine any of them doing something like that. I'd known them all a long time, and I trusted them. Well, all except for Ephy. It wasn't that I didn't trust her—I just didn't know her yet. Still, I didn't think she could have possibly... no, she couldn't have.

That meant it had to be someone who came to the party. Someone had come to the party under the pretense of celebrating with us but had poisoned us instead. I couldn't imagine who could have done such a thing. Who among my friends and neighbors would do that?

I held out a fragile hope that something had come in from a vendor already contaminated, but it seemed unlikely. I'd tasted everything as I made it and hadn't gotten sick until the party itself. Maybe there was still a chance it hadn't been someone at the party.

A tech stuck his head out of the back room. "What do you want us to get from back here, Detective? She's got a lot of stuff."

I bristled at his choice of words. As if I'd somehow intentionally made sure I was well-stocked with supplies, just to annoy them or make their jobs more difficult.

Mike rubbed his forehead and looked at me. "What do you have back there?"

The rebellious side of me wanted to blurt out that I had poison, of course, but I didn't think Mike would see the humor in it. I chose the wiser option. "Supplies. Some extra food I had for the party."

He nodded. "Get samples of all the party food in the—" He looked at me again.

"Fridge."

"In the fridge."

The tech nodded and walked back into the kitchen. As he went, I realized I actually did have poison on site, if you considered cleaning products a potential poison, which I supposed they were if they were put into someone's food. And then I thought of something else. I'd been so focused on the "who" that I hadn't even thought about the "what."

"What kind of poison was it?"

Mike looked down at me with his eyebrow raised like he wasn't sure I was talking to him.

"You said the food was poisoned, but you didn't say what the poison was."

He grunted and turned back to watch the techs still going through every last inch of the café.

"You're not going to tell me?"

"I don't think that would be a good idea at this stage in the investigation," he said without looking at me.

"Why? Are you afraid I'll accidentally tip someone off?" And then a worse possibility crossed my mind. "You don't actually think I had something to do with it, do you?"

Mike crossed his arms over his chest and glanced down at me out of the corner of his eye before looking back at the techs.

I sank back in my chair as a fresh wave of nausea washed over me. Since Mike announced that someone had poisoned my guests, I'd reassured myself with the thought that Mike knew me and understood that I would never do anything like that. But now I wasn't so sure. And that terrified me.

Chapter 10

WE WERE BACK at my house when Mike walked into the living room. The crime scene techs had finished at the café and done a quick search of Matt's house before coming to mine and settling in for what looked like the long haul. They'd already been through my kitchen cabinets and drawers, and now techs were digging through my refrigerator, pantry, dresser drawers, and bathroom. Two of them were even sitting on the floor in the bedroom that used to be my grandparents', going through the boxes I'd packed up with their belongings. To keep myself from freaking out about it all, I kept telling myself that they would put everything neatly away when they were finished, even if I wasn't sure that it was true.

"How you holding up?" he asked, leaning on the doorframe.

I took a deep breath and turned to look at him from my place on the couch. My first instinct had been to snap back with some smart-alecky comment about how he was suddenly acting like he wanted to be my friend again, but before I could say anything, I noticed how utterly miserable he looked. He was my friend, even if we were on opposing sides of an investigation at the moment.

"You look terrible. Do you want to sit down?" I gestured at the chair nearby.

He looked at the chair with something like longing, paused for a moment, then lowered himself down into it. He rested his head on the back of the chair and closed his eyes. My own eyelids started to feel heavy—well, heav*ier*, since I'd been one pillow away from falling asleep all day. Now, seeing Mike looking like he was drifting off, I was starting to think I didn't need a pillow at all. Wouldn't it be just as easy to fall asleep sitting up? Or maybe to rest my head on the arm of the couch. That seemed like a good idea.

Just as I started to lean over, Mike's eyes opened. "Almost fell asleep there," he said, blinking rapidly.

I righted myself and pulled my blanket tighter

around my shoulders. I couldn't wait for all this to be over, if only so that I could go to sleep for a while. "I was hoping you would so that I could take a nap."

He chuckled then winced and rubbed his head. "Head's killing me," he muttered.

"Your eyes are all red."

"Are they?" He rubbed both eyes with the heels of his hands. "You have any of those anti-redness eye drops?"

I resisted shaking my head, knowing how much it would hurt. "Nope."

His eyebrows rose ever so slightly. "You sure?"

What a strange question. Why would I lie about something like that? Why would he even *think* that I would lie about something like that? "Yes, I'm sure. Why do you ask?"

Mike sighed and looked down at his lap. He rubbed at his fingernails with his thumb. "You hear what happens if someone puts some of those into your drink?" he asked, watching me out of the corner of his eye.

"I think I saw it in a movie once. It gives you an upset stomach or something, right?"

He bit his lip and rubbed the back of his hand across his stubbled chin—another sign that he wasn't feeling well. I'd never seen him with so much as a five o'clock shadow before. "It's a lot more than an upset stomach. Headache, tremors, blurred vision, trouble breathing, messes with your blood pressure..." He trailed off, his eyes still fixed on my face as my eyes went wide.

"You mean that's—someone put eye drops—you're joking, right?"

Mike slowly shook his head. "I wish I was."

I leaned back on the couch, trying to wrap my head around it. It was so bizarre to think of someone doing that—slipping eye drops into the food. And then to think of something so common, so innocuous, making so many people so sick. "Could it have been an accident?"

"Have you ever accidentally added eye drops to food at a party?"

"Of course not."

He bobbed his head. "Exactly."

I shook my head as much as I could without sending pain radiating up through my skull. "You're sure about his?"

"Unfortunately." He pulled his notebook out of his pants pocket and flipped it open. "Tetrahydrozoline." He pronounced each syllable separately as he stumbled through the unfamiliar word. "Anti-redness drops. So I take it we're not going to find any of those?"

"Nope." At least I hoped not. I never used them, but I wasn't completely certain that my mother or grandparents hadn't used any and tucked the bottle in some forgotten corner. I hoped the long-past expiration date would be enough to convince the investigators the drops weren't mine.

"Didn't think so." Mike rested his head against the back of the chair again and let out a slow, deep breath. "I'm sorry to be putting you through all this. You had the most access to all the food, so I have to rule you out before I can move on to other suspects."

"You have other suspects?"

"Only about a hundred of them. How many people did you have at this shindig anyway? It was an open house, wasn't it? Do you even know how many people showed up?"

"Not exactly. We had sort of a sign-in sheet, but I don't know who signed in or didn't."

Mike's eyes lit up with interest. "Can I get a copy of that?"

"It's back at the café, but you're welcome to it."

He scribbled something down in his notebook. "I'll need you to look it over and see if you notice anyone's missing, but I don't expect you to get it a hundred percent."

He said it, but I didn't necessarily believe that he meant it. Mike could be a little snippy when things didn't go his way. I was sure he *thought* he meant it anyway.

Mike drummed the end of his pen on his notebook. "You notice anyone acting suspicious last night? Doing anything unusual?"

"Like putting eye drops into the food?"

He shrugged. "If that's what you saw."

I shook my head before remembering how much that hurt. I winced and held my breath until the wave of pain subsided. Holding my head in my hand, I finally got out an answer. "I've been wracking my brain trying to think of anything, but I can't. I can't think of anything unusual at all." Out of the blue, the image of Ephy lurking by the food table, sipping her glass of water, came to mind. But drinking a glass of water wasn't a crime. There was no reason to mention that to Mike.

"I think that's the tetra——" He looked down at his notebook and blinked hard. "The eye drops wracking your brain." Mike chuckled weakly.

I managed something like a smile. "What about

you? You were there. Did you see anyone acting suspicious?"

"Fran, I'm not at liberty to discuss—"

"Mike, you're literally discussing an active investigation with me right now. Besides, I'm not asking you as the detective investigating the case. I'm asking you as my friend who came to my birthday party."

Mike shifted in his chair and looked at me like he wasn't sure if my motives were entirely pure. He was probably worrying that I was going to try to solve the case myself. It wasn't a completely unfounded concern, but I was way too sick to be thinking about that. All that was on my mind at that moment was a nap, some ibuprofen, and the current tenuous state of my stomach.

He finally sighed and shook his head slightly. "I wish I did." He pressed his lips together. "I'm just hoping something clicks into place during this investigation. Something that seemed insignificant suddenly becomes the key to the whole case."

Like Ephy and her water. But that was ridiculous. People were allowed to drink water at a party. And her objection—that she didn't like sweet stuff— made sense. There were a lot of sweets at the party. *But she gave you that sugar cookie recipe.* Knowing a great sugar cookie recipe didn't mean anything. Everybody liked a cookie now and again, didn't they? Plus, maybe she just didn't like to drink sweet things. Between the sorbet, the pineapple juice, and the soda, the punch really was on the sugary side. That was probably all she meant. It had to be.

"So what comes next?" I asked.

"Well, unless these guys find a receipt for a major eye drop purchase around here, I'll move on to the next most obvious suspects." He glanced at me and saw the question on my face. He took a deep breath. "I'm going to need to talk to your employees."

If it was possible, I sank farther into the couch. I hated my girls being dragged this, even if I understood why they were his next targets. "Then what?" I asked, wondering whether it would get better or somehow worse.

"Then—" He hesitated. "Then we go through the guest list."

"And what? Search everyone's houses until you find someone who has a problem with their eyes getting red?"

He gave me a look that I could only describe as disdain. I knew why. I was being sarcastic when he was just trying to do his job.

"We'll try to identify who might have had a motive."

"What kind of motive would someone have to poison a hundred or so people? Can there even be a motive for that?"

He sighed. "There's always a motive. Even if it's just because they think it would be fun to cause havoc."

I was incredulous. "Seriously? You think someone could have done this just for fun? What kind of sick person would poison one hundred people just for fun?"

He shrugged. "We don't know if that was what it was, Fran. It could be anything. It could have been just a way to cause trouble, or they could have been targeting one person and everyone else was collateral damage. We just don't know. But that's why we're investigating—to find out who would have done this and why."

It made sense, but it was torture. I wanted the solution to be simple and easy. I wanted there to be an obvious suspect—someone who wasn't one of my nearest and dearest—and I wanted them to have a good reason for having done it, although I couldn't imagine what kind of good reason anyone could have for pouring eye drops into the food at my party. Or maybe it was an accident. It would have to be a pretty crazy accident, though.

I took a deep breath. It hadn't even been a day, but I was ready for this to be over and for everything to get back to normal. I wanted to forget that it had ever happened.

"When can I reopen the café?" I asked. There would be a ton of cleanup to do before we could get back to business as usual, and I was anxious to get it started as soon as possible.

Mike made a face. "Not until we get all the test results back and figure out what food the poison was added to. We may have to come back for more samples of the ones we took for the tetra—uh, the eye drops."

"So I can't even go clean up?"

"Sorry, Fran. You're just going to have to be patient until we get all our loose ends tied up."

I made a face. I was good at many things, but being patient wasn't one of them.

Mike caught my eye and chuckled. "I know that's not your strong suit, but I believe in you."

Before I could think up a saucy comeback, one of the techs stuck her head around the doorframe. "Detective? We're ready for you."

Mike moved to get up, stopped, and then

started back up more slowly. He followed her around the corner.

One advantage of having a small house—one I definitely hadn't appreciated growing up there as a teenager—was that you could hear almost everything from anywhere.

"Find anything?" Mike asked, quietly but definitely still within earshot.

I held my breath, worried even though I knew I'd had nothing to do with the poisoning.

"Nothing at all out of the ordinary, sir," the tech replied.

I let out my breath and rested my head on the back of the couch. I was in the clear. Now I just had to hope Mike found out who the real culprit was—and fast too. I still felt terrible, but I wanted to return to work the second I was back on my feet. The very moment he told me I could go back in the café, if possible. Yes, that was what I wanted. But until then, a nap sounded like just the thing.

Chapter 11

I WAS FEELING BETTER by the time I woke up from my nap. Not *good*, mind you, but better than I was. My head only ached a little, and my stomach had calmed to the point where I could almost stand the thought of eating something. Almost. As appealing as a cup of coffee sounded in theory—especially given my headache—my stomach still turned at the very thought of swallowing anything. But at least I could sit up straight and think clearly.

Of course, that meant my brain could now form coherent thoughts about the party and the poisoning. And the first one was that I needed to know what food had been poisoned. Maybe if I figured that out, I could figure out who had done it. Not that I had any intention of getting involved with Mike's investigation. I was more than happy to leave that up to him. But since it was my food and my café, I was the best person to spot anything out of the ordinary. I wouldn't do any investigating, just some observing. And I'd report anything out of the ordinary to Mike immediately. What could possibly be the harm? I'd go to the café, take a look around, and see if anything stood out. He told me I couldn't clean up or open up, but he didn't say I had to stay out.

But first, I needed to call Matt. And then I needed to take a shower. For one thing, I knew I could really use one—and a good teeth-brushing. On top of that, I felt like it would be a good test of how much better I was actually feeling. After all, my mother had always said that if you could make it through a shower, you could make it through the day and, for the most part, I'd found that she was right. If I could get through my shower, I could get through my day.

I grabbed my phone and called Matt. He grunted hello just before it went to voicemail. "You okay?" I asked.

He groaned.

"Did I wake you up?"

"Uh-huh," he said with a moan.

"Do you want me to let you go back to sleep?"

"Uh-huh."

I said goodbye and let him go back to sleep then headed up the stairs to get cleaned up. I checked my closet and drawers to see what kind of damage the crime scene techs had done. It wasn't as bad as it could have been, all things considered. I could tell someone had rustled through the clothes, but everything was still sort of folded and roughly where it had been. I opened my underwear drawer and reached for a clean pair then pulled my hand back. Someone—I didn't know who—had been digging through it only a couple of hours earlier. Who knew what they'd touched just before or if they'd washed their hands? What if they'd just opened up the toilet tank or checked the cleaning chemicals under the vanity? I scooped up every last scrap of fabric in the drawer and dumped it all in the hamper. I'd figure something out, but I wasn't going to put on anything that some stranger had just had their filthy hands on.

I survived my shower and scrounged up some clothes that hadn't obviously been pawed over. Latte was over at Matt's, probably curled up next to him on the bed, keeping Matt's legs warm whether he wanted him to or not. I would have enjoyed those snuggles during my own nap, but Matt had sounded like he was worse off than I was, so I didn't mind. I locked up the house and headed for the café.

This time, I went in the back door instead of the front. It was a slightly shorter walk to go that way, and I wanted to conserve my energy just in case the positive effects of my nap wore off. Plus, it wasn't as easily noticeable from the street if I used that entrance. Mike might not have told me to stay away from the café, but I didn't want to tempt his wrath by strolling down Main Street and through the front door. He'd probably claim I should have known to stay away, but I didn't see how he could really blame me if he hadn't told me to keep out. I was allowed to be in my house, wasn't I? Why not also the café? Even so, it seemed safer to sneak—I mean to *go* in through the back.

It was eerily quiet inside and not just because I was alone. I spent a lot of time alone in the café. There were many times that I stayed late after closing to bake or get some paperwork done. It was plenty quiet then, but somehow this was different. I found myself peeking under every table and behind every closed door in the place—even the bathrooms' closed doors, which I immediately wished I hadn't looked behind. My stomach turned, and I had to stand stock-still for a minute until the wave of nausea the smell brought on had passed. I'd have to see if I could hire someone with a stronger stomach to clean it up for me—when Mike granted permission, of course.

I walked over to the tables that were still half full of food from the party—food that had now been picked over by party guests and crime scene techs. For the most part, it looked... fine. I'd been around food enough in my life to recognize that the puff pastry dishes had gotten a little soggy, the cookies weren't quite as soft or crisp as they should be, and the punch had been untouched and uncovered for too long, but nothing gave me any visual indication that anything had been poisoned. I don't know what I expected poisoned food to look like, of course—maybe a skull and crossbones or Poison Control Mr. Yuk imprinted on them—but whatever it was, I didn't see it.

I leaned down to get a closer look at everything, on my guard like the food was a spider that could see me coming and jump at my face. Fortunately, nothing moved.

I reached out and picked up one of the Italian sausage canapés to examine it more closely. I even sniffed it, but it just smelled like cold, day-old sausage and butter. I put it down and moved on down the table, picking up one or two pieces from each tray, looking them over, and smelling them. Aside from being stale, nothing seemed out of the ordinary in the slightest. Even the plates, cups, and napkins—one of which someone had taken the time to fold into an intricate design—that had been left behind all looked like perfectly normal trash.

I sat down in a chair at the front of the café to figure out my next move. Almost immediately, I was jolted out of my thoughts by someone knocking on the window next to my head. Instantly, I knew it was Mike. I was caught, and now I'd have to endure, at best, a dirty look and, at worst, a lecture on how I needed to stay out of police business and mind my own. Of course, in a quite literal sense, I *was* minding my business, but I didn't think Mike would appreciate that argument.

I took a deep breath before turning to face his judgement.

But instead of Mike's eyes glaring down at me from beneath his crew cut, I saw Melissa with a big smile on her face as she waved at me. I hopped up from my chair and unlocked the door to let her in.

She threw her arms around me as best she could with her pregnant belly between us.

"I heard what happened! It's terrible! I'm so sorry! Are you okay? How are you feeling?" She had each of my hands grasped in one of hers and looked at me with genuine concern in her eyes.

"I'm okay. A lot better than I was this morning, that's for sure." It suddenly dawned on me that that as miserable as I'd been, Melissa would have felt so much more miserable than I did—not to mention how bad the drug in the eye drops would have been for her baby. "But what about you? How are you feeling?"

"Oh, I'm fine!" she said, her blue eyes sparkling. She really looked the part of the glowing expectant mother. "I don't know how, since I'm pretty sure I had at least two of every single thing on the table, so I must have eaten some of whatever was bad. This little girl's a hungry one!" She patted her belly and laughed. "But maybe she gives me some kind of protection from food poisoning."

I realized then that she didn't know about the poison—only that people had gotten sick. But still, she hadn't gotten sick. "You ate some of everything?"

Melissa nodded, setting her dark curls bouncing

while she eyed the food still on the tables. She looked like she was barely holding herself back from heading over and loading up another plate. "It wasn't like this at all with Emmy. I barely ate anything with her. Pretty much everything grossed me out. I'm like a bottomless pit with this one. First time in my life my eyes haven't been bigger than my stomach!" She giggled, rubbing her belly affectionately.

"And you didn't get sick at all?"

She shook her head. "Nope, not at all! Like I said, I guess the baby must have given me some kind of food poisoning protection or something."

"Melissa—" I stepped closer and lowered my voice, even though I knew we were completely alone. "I don't want to freak you out or anything, but it wasn't food poisoning."

Her unlined forehead wrinkled. "What do you mean? What made everyone sick if it wasn't the food?"

I took a deep breath, still not sure if I should really tell her what had actually happened. Mike hadn't said I couldn't, but he hadn't said I could either. Of course, I hadn't let that ambiguity keep me out of the café, so why should I let it keep me from telling Melissa about the poison? "It was the food," I said quietly. "But it was something someone put in the food on purpose. It was poison."

She looked at me for a moment, blinking, her forehead still wrinkled. "It was—it was *poison?*" Both arms wrapped protectively around her middle. "What—who—why—*what?*" Her lower lip began to tremble.

I put my arm around her and pulled her toward me to comfort her. "I know. It's crazy. They don't know who did it yet or why, but the police are investigating."

Her eyes welled up. "But *poison!* We're lucky no one died! Oh my God, someone could have died. I could have died! My baby—!" She covered her face with her hands as she dissolved into tears. I put my other arm around her, too, and held her until her tears had calmed and she wiped her eyes with the backs of her hands. I stepped over to the table and grabbed a couple napkins for her to use.

She dabbed at her eyes, wiped her nose, and struggled through a couple of deep breaths punctuated by her fading sobs. "I—I just can't believe it. It's so scary."

I nodded. "That was why I asked if you were sure you ate some of everything. If you didn't get sick, the poison must have been in something you didn't eat."

She nodded and turned her red, swollen eyes towards the table. Wordlessly, she crossed to the far end of the table with the non-alcoholic punch and started walking down it, pointing at each tray and nodding as she went. She got to the end and turned toward me, looking like she was ready to burst into tears again. "I had some of everything."

I sighed and rubbed my hands up and down my face. "So much for that theory," I muttered. If Melissa had some of everything and didn't get sick at all, that meant the poison might have been added to individual servings. And if the poison had been added to individual servings, it was possible that none of the samples the crime scene techs had taken would turn out positive for the poison. And who knew what that would do to the investigation? Probably blow the whole thing up. Or make them turn on me again.

"I'm so sorry." Melissa wiped her eyes again. "Everything just looked so good! I couldn't help myself!"

I went over to comfort her again. It wasn't her fault, of course, and I felt bad for making a pregnant woman cry. As I put my arms around her, my eyes fell on the punch bowl on this end of the table. Spiked on this end, non-alcoholic on the other. "Wait! Melissa! You didn't have some of everything!"

"Yes, I did," she said, sniffling.

"No, you didn't." I turned her around gently and pointed at the bowl of the spiked punch.

"Yes, I—" She stopped, and her eyes grew wide. "No, I didn't! I didn't have everything. I didn't have the alcoholic punch."

Her voice came out in a squeal, and she clapped her hands a couple of times. She had a massive grin on her face as she bounced up and down on the balls of her feet. She'd gone from happy to devastated and back to happy again in a manner of minutes. The wonders of pregnancy, I assumed.

"That's right," I mumbled, more to myself than to her. "And neither did Becky or Amanda, and they didn't get sick either. Or Ephy." I met Melissa's eyes. "It was the punch. Someone poisoned the punch."

Chapter 12

I HAD my phone out to dial Mike before Melissa even had time to swing from excitement about our discovery back to distress about what had happened.

"Yeah?" Mike said by way of greeting.

"Well, hello to you, too, Officer." As eager as I was to tell Mike what Melissa and I had figured out, I wasn't about to let him get away with being rude.

"It's 'Detective.'" He would have sounded stern if he hadn't chuckled quietly first. He must have been feeling better. "What's up? I was just on my way to see you."

My heart skipped and not in a good way either. It was in a bad way. A very bad way. "Oh. Um, where?"

"Where?" He sounded genuinely confused. "At your house? You're at home, aren't you? Or did you go back to Matt's?" His turn signal clicked in the background. He was already on his way to my house, and I wasn't there. I was at the café, which was the worst possible place I could be if Mike was looking for me.

I thought fast, trying to decide whether it was best to meet Mike back at my place or Matt's. I wanted to check up on Matt and could have really used some of Latte's kisses, but I was afraid Matt would accidentally give it away that I hadn't been there all afternoon. Not that I thought I'd done anything wrong by going to the café. I just didn't want to have to deal with explaining it to Mike.

"Oh, yeah, my house. I just wasn't sure if I was supposed to meet you somewhere." I chose my words carefully to keep from straight-out lying.

Melissa's head jerked up, and she looked at me curiously. I pressed my lips together and gave her a little wave to let her know I'd explain in a minute.

"Can you just give me ten minutes or so to let me get cleaned up a little?" Again, not a lie per se. It would be good to run a cool washcloth over my face and neck. I wasn't sure whether it was the lingering effects of the eye drops or if someone had turned the café's air conditioning off, but I was starting to feel warm and a little clammy.

"Yeah, that's fine. I could use a cup of coff—" He stopped and groaned. "I forgot you're closed. I'm going to have to get gas station coffee." His disgust practically walked through the phone to shake hands with me.

"I can make you some when I—when you get to my house."

Mike sighed. "I'll see if I can hold out."

He didn't sound sure that he could, and to be honest, neither was I. This morning while he supervised the search was the longest I'd ever seen him go without pouring hot coffee down his throat. I didn't know if he'd gotten a hold of any since then, but I did know that ten minutes was a long time for him to wait after he'd decided he needed a cup. I'd have to think about whether to have mercy on him if he showed up at my house carrying some gas station sludge. It was usually an easy decision to give him as much coffee as he wanted as often as he wanted, but he didn't usually spend the morning searching my house and business.

"Okay! I'll see you soon," I chirped. Then I hung up.

Melissa looked at me like she thought I'd lost my mind.

I smiled weakly. "That was Mike Stanton. From the police department. I'm not sure if he's okay with me being here while the investigation is still ongoing."

She nodded knowingly. She was a sweet girl, but I had a feeling she had her rebellious side too.

"He'll be at my house in ten minutes, so I need to get out of here and get back home."

"Are you going to tell him about the punch?" she asked, moving toward the door.

I was almost afraid to let her out through the front in case Mike drove by, but it didn't seem fair to ask her to go out the back and have to walk all the way around the building to get back to the sidewalk and the street.

"Absolutely. Hopefully it will help them solve the case."

Maybe knowing it was the spiked punch would help them identify who had the most access—other than me, of course. I didn't know how it would help them, but I held out hope that it somehow would.

"I hope so. I hate even thinking about someone doing such a thing and still being out on the streets where they could hurt someone else." Melissa shuddered and held her pregnant belly again.

I opened the door for her.

"Let me know if there's any way I can help. I can't do much of anything physical lugging this little one around, but I'm still good at sitting and eating if you need me to eavesdrop on anyone." She giggled, making her eyes sparkle and her dimples pop out.

"You're welcome to come over and volunteer your services anytime." I laughed at first, but it faded as something came to mind. "Actually, you didn't see anything suspicious last night, did you?"

Melissa thought for a moment, inclining her head and pursing her lips. She shook her head and shrugged. "No, I don't think so."

"What about someone hanging around the food or the punch bowl? Did you see anything like that?"

She thought again, started to shake her head, then stopped with her forehead wrinkled. "Well, actually…" She trailed off, still looking thoughtful. "Never mind, it was probably nothing."

"Anything you saw could help. The way Mike was talking, anybody could be a suspect."

"I don't want to get anyone in trouble."

Fearing I'd spooked her, I rushed to smooth it

over. "No, no. You wouldn't be getting anyone in trouble. The police are going to talk to everyone who was here last night anyway. Anything you saw would just be helping them know who to start with."

She still looked uneasy. "I was up there a lot, you know. That's what other people might have been doing too."

I nodded. "Of course. Like I said, it's just to help the police figure out who else might know something."

She hesitated then took a deep breath. "There was a girl. I don't think I've seen her before. She had dark hair. Kind of purplish? She was standing right over there against the wall by the punch bowl pretty much the whole time."

Ephy.

"And Todd from Todd's Gym was up there with Karli. You know her, don't you? She works the front desk at the gym? They were having some kind of really intense-looking conversation for a while. They were right there, on the other side of the table." She pointed at the far side of the table, close to the counter. "And then that guy from the jewelry store —you know, the one who always wears his hair slicked back?"

I nodded. "Dean Howard. He's the owner."

"Yeah, him. He was lurking around there some. I don't really know what he was doing. I just had to scoot by him a few times."

I glanced over at the big wrought-iron clock on the exposed-brick wall and realized I would have to hustle if I was going to make it home before Mike arrived on my doorstep. "I don't want to rush you—"

"Oh, no, I get it," she chirped, waving me off. She started back towards the door.

I thanked her for coming by and gave her a quick hug before she headed out. I let her have a few seconds to get a little ways down the sidewalk to make sure she didn't think I was desperate to get rid of her. Then I shut the door and locked it. I hesitated for a second, wondering if I should grab the guest list, but decided against it, since doing that would be a dead giveaway that I'd been there. I hustled out the back and across the parking lot behind the buildings on Main Street.

I needed to get home as soon as possible, but I also needed not to kill myself in the process. If I pushed too hard, I'd probably collapse in somebody's yard and have to take another nap before I could finish making my way home. I could just see myself waking up to Mike's less-than-happy face staring down at me sprawled out on a neighbor's grass. He'd want an explanation for sure, and my eye-drop-addled brain wouldn't come up with anything other than the truth—that I'd been at the café, literally sniffing around. And that was the last thing I wanted to tell him.

Even though I did have Melissa's comments about seeing Ephy hanging around the punch bowl ringing in my ears.

Chapter 13

I TOOK my old childhood shortcut across the back-yards on my street, hoping it would give me enough of an edge to beat Mike. It felt a little odd to be a fully grown, very almost-thirty-five-year-old woman tramping through people's yards—especially since I'd found a body the last time I did it—but I was willing to risk feeling silly to avoid having to explain my trip to the café.

I was just crossing over into my backyard when I saw Mike's car pull up in front of my house. I broke into a jog and immediately regretted it. Before I'd gone five feet, I was panting and light-headed. Somehow, I still managed to make it to and through my back door just as Mike knocked at the front. As much as I wanted to collapse on the couch, I forced myself to the door and pulled it open with a big, fake smile on my face.

I regretted it as soon as I did. That kind of smile would make Mike immediately suspicious. He would know something was up, figure out what it was, and find a way to prove it if I tried to deny it. It would have been better if I'd just been late.

"Hey, Fran. Mind if I come in and sit down?" Coming from a police officer who was investigating a poisoning case I may or may not have been a suspect in, those words should have been intimidating. But between Mike's glassy eyes and the way he swayed slightly on my doorstep, intimidation was the last thing I was feeling.

"Yeah, of course, come in." I stepped back and held the door for him to get by.

He sank into the closest chair, put his head back, and closed his eyes.

"Are you okay?" I was relieved he hadn't noticed my fake smile or that I was still out of breath from my brief jog, but I was also concerned. For one thing, he hadn't noticed either of those obvious things. He also looked somehow worse than he had that morning. Probably because he'd been running around all day, trying to solve the case, instead of taking a three-hour nap like I had.

Mike grunted and waved his hand. "I just need a minute," he muttered. "I'll be fine."

I went to the kitchen to make some ginger tea.

Tea wasn't exactly my thing. It hadn't been my mom or my grandparents' thing, either, which was why I'd had to spend days researching different brands, varieties, and brewing techniques before I was comfortable serving any tea other than what came from some dusty old grocery store teabags after a lovely old British couple asked me for some one day. Now, although I could talk for a solid fifteen minutes on proper brewing temperatures, I still didn't really drink tea. The same way some poor souls inexplicably weren't coffee fans, I couldn't fall in love with tea, no matter how much milk, sugar, syrup, or honey I did or didn't add to it.

But ginger tea was a different story. Both my mother and grandmother had been devotees of ginger tea for all sorts of things but upset stomachs especially. Any time I'd so much as mentioned my stomach bothering me while I was growing up, a cup of ginger tea would appear as if by magic beside me. I hadn't been much of a fan of it—its warm, spicy flavor had been too much for me as a kid. I'd gotten used to it, though, and now I found it comforting, especially when my stomach was bothering me.

I pulled my ginger out of the refrigerator, grabbed a hand grater, and started grating it. Ginger tea the way the *famiglia Amaro* made it wasn't a true tea, of course, since we didn't use tea leaves, just grated ginger steeped in water with a touch of honey for sweetness. Normally, I would let the tea brew for about ten minutes before serving it, but I didn't think I could stand that long and doubted I'd be getting up anytime soon once I sat. So, I put the ginger into a couple of tea balls, plunked them into mugs, filled them from the water tap on the espresso machine, added a couple drops of honey in each, and carried them to the living room. I put one on the end table next to Mike and curled up on the couch with the other.

He opened his eyes just enough for me to see them flick over at the mug. "No. No coffee."

I was suddenly even more concerned. "Do you need to go home and go to bed?"

"No, I just—" He made a disgusted face. "I stopped at the gas station. Their coffee's gotten worse since the last time I was there. I don't think they clean the pots. Maybe I should send the health department over." He closed his eyes and rested his head back on the chair.

"Well, it's not coffee anyway. It's ginger tea."

If it was possible, he looked even more disgusted. "Thanks, but I'll pass."

"It'll help your stomach. Trust me." I made a show of taking a big sip from my mug, even though the ginger hadn't steeped enough, and I wasn't sure Mike's eyes were open to see it. In fact, based on the way his breathing was slowing, I was pretty sure he was asleep.

I let him be. He clearly needed the rest, and I could use the time to think. Unfortunately, the first thought that crossed my mind was Ephy standing by the punch bowl, sipping her water. Was she hovering so that she could dump eye drops in the punch bowl or for some other reason? What other reason could she have? Maybe she just didn't enjoy big social events and preferred to hang out on the edges. Maybe. Or maybe she was as mad at the world as her clothes suggested. I sighed.

Mike stirred in his chair but didn't wake up—or at least didn't let on that he was awake.

I sipped my tea. It was perfect. I swirled the tea ball around in the mug, pulled it out and laid it on a napkin on the end table, then did the same for Mike's cup.

"That stuff will really help my stomach?" Mike opened one eye and turned it towards me.

"Yup." I took a sip from my mug to make my point.

He heaved a sigh and looked at the mug on the table next to him. He looked skeptical but picked up the mug and brought it to his lips. He made a face but didn't complain, so I took it as a win. "So, I managed to pull some strings over at the lab, and we have the preliminary results back on the food from the party."

"It was the punch, wasn't it?" The words exploded out of my mouth before I realized what a bad idea it was to say them out loud.

Mike's right eyebrow went up. He stared at me silently, which of course made me nervous.

"I saw Melissa," I blurted out. "I think you know her. She was at the party last night. The pregnant one?"

Mike's face didn't so much as twitch.

"Anyway, I talked to her, and I was worried

because of the baby, but she was *fine*, not sick at all, even though she ate some of everything. Everything *except* the punch. The spiked punch, I mean. She had the regular punch, which is how we figured out what it was."

Mike took another sip of his tea without taking his eyes off me. "You just happened to run into Melissa." It was a statement, not a question, even though his disbelief was clear.

"Yes, I did," I said, more than a little proud that I wasn't just telling Mike what he wanted to hear but also being completely truthful.

"Here in the house?" Now both eyebrows were up, and he was looking at me the way he probably looked at his kids when they tried to tell him some far-fetched lie about how it hadn't been *them* that climbed on top of the dresser and dumped out Mommy's jewelry box—it had been the dog, yeah, the dog.

"No, I, um—I went out for a little bit. To get some fresh air."

"Whe—" He stopped, shut his eyes, and shook his head. "Never mind. I don't want to know." He squeezed the bridge of his nose and took a deep breath then a sip of his tea. "I'd say you missed your calling, but I've had your coffee, and I'm not sure you did."

I snapped my hand to my heart and gasped. "Was that a compliment, Mike?"

"Don't get excited. I'm sick. I don't know what I'm saying."

I chuckled to myself. It was the closest thing I'd get to a compliment on my detective skills from him. He barely even gave them out for my coffee and baking, and I knew he enjoyed those.

He swallowed down some more of his tea. "Now that you know it was the punch and you've had a chance to chat with your friend about it, have you thought of anything that might be suspicious? Or just worth mentioning to the person actually in charge of this case?"

Ephy.

He looked at me with the kind of piercing look that made me wonder if he could read my mind.

I felt bad, like I was lying to him if I didn't tell him about Ephy. I wasn't, though. Not really. I didn't have any specific reason to suspect her—just a nagging thought in the back of my mind. And that wasn't nearly enough of a reason to turn her in to the police, especially not when that nagging thought probably had more to do with my bad first impression of her than anything she'd done the night of the party.

He was still looking at me, waiting for my answer.

"No. Nothing at all."

Chapter 14

WITH THE POISONED food identified and all the punch ingredients disposed of, Mike gave me the name of a good cleaning company and permission to reopen the café.

I was a little hesitant to call up a company called Crime Scene Clean-Up, particularly since the motto emblazoned across their website was "Blood, Guts & Goo—We'll Clean it All for You!" But I didn't think I could literally or figuratively stomach cleaning the café to the extent it needed to be, even if I called all the girls in to help. Or maybe especially not if they helped, since I knew Rhonda and Sammy were still feeling queasy.

Mike had assured me that this company was the best and fast to boot, so I sucked it up and called them. The girl who answered the phone sounded almost disappointed when I told her that very few bodily fluids needed to be cleaned up and they were all confined to the bathrooms. Apparently, stale food and fingerprint dust weren't the most exciting things to clean. Still, she assured me that a team would be out within the hour, and they'd have everything cleaned up and ready to go for the café to reopen in the morning.

Sure enough, when I walked in just before dawn the next morning, the place was immaculate. It somehow didn't even smell like cleaning chemicals like I'd expected—it was why I'd gotten there extra early—so I could prop the doors open and air the place out before customers came in. Whatever the cleaners had used, though, left the place smelling fresh more than anything. And soon, I planned to have the mouthwatering aroma of fresh-brewed coffee floating on the air, which I did by the time Sammy walked in.

"I was about to call the police until I saw you behind the counter. Are you okay? Why are you here so early?" Sammy walked in through the door I'd decided to prop open after all as a kind of advertisement that we were open again. Aside from a pinker-than-usual flush to her cheeks, she looked like she was back to her usual self.

I laughed. "Just wanted to make sure everything was looking good and ready for us to open." I opened my arms and gave her a hug as she walked around the counter to me.

Sammy put her head to my forehead. "Are you sure? This is awfully early for you." She stopped and chuckled. "It's even early for me! I thought I'd have some cleaning up to do before we opened."

I made her a cup of coffee as we chatted about how we were feeling, and I updated her on the police investigation so far.

"Do they have any suspects?" She cradled her coffee cup in her hands and breathed in its smell.

"I don't think they do."

For the thousandth time, I wondered if I should have mentioned Ephy's behavior at the party to Mike. And then I wondered if I should mention it to Sammy. On the one hand, her boyfriend was a police officer, but on the other, she knew Ephy as well as I did and would have a good perspective. Plus, she thought the absolute best of people until they had proven that they really didn't deserve it, and even then she wouldn't give up on them entirely. In the end, my anxiety over whether I was doing the right thing won out over the risk she'd spill everything to Ryan.

"Actually, about that—can I ask you something?"

"Of course! Anything." She gave me her patented bright Sammy smile.

"This is probably crazy, but—" I stopped to wonder one last time whether it was a good idea to tell her. Then I blurted it out. "Ephy spent the whole party leaning against the wall over there, right next to the poisoned punch. And she was drinking water the whole time because she 'doesn't like sweet stuff.' But I've seen her eat sweet things here at the café, haven't you? I don't know whether this is really something you should tell Mike or if I'm just jumping to conclusions because she can be abrasive sometimes."

Sammy nodded slowly and chewed on her lip. "I think—" She stopped, and her forehead wrinkled. She took a long, deep breath. "I think you should tell Mike. But not that you think she may have had something to do with it—just that you saw her by the punch bowl and maybe she saw something that would help. I think that's most likely what could have happened anyway. I can't imagine our Ephy poisoning anyone, but she could have seen something and not even realized that it was important, especially since people didn't start getting sick until later."

I wanted to hug her. In fact, I did. I couldn't believe such an obvious solution had been sitting there all along, and I'd just been so busy thinking about the possibility that she'd poisoned everyone that it didn't even occur to me that she might not have done anything but seen someone do something instead. It felt like a weight had been lifted off my shoulders. And just in time, too, because our first customer of the day walked through the door.

"Good morning, Mr. Paul!" Sammy called, flashing that smile again. "How are you on this beautiful day? The usual?"

She had such a way with customers that my mind held no doubt that she was a large part of the café's success, especially in the early morning hours when most people were grumpy and surly. Sammy, by contrast, was like a ray of sunshine then, bouncing around the café and making everything and everyone a little brighter.

As Sammy moved to start making his coffee—an order she knew by heart, just like she did with all the regulars—I stepped over to her. "I'm going to go make some muffins. Thanks again."

She nodded, and I hurried into the back. Virtually nothing in the pastry case could be saved after being closed for a whole day. I had to make everything fresh. I preferred to make everything fresh anyway, but I didn't mind leaving a few things that kept well an extra day. Today, though, I'd have to remake almost everything, especially since I knew that hungry customers would be coming in and looking for their breakfast at any moment.

Muffins seemed like just the thing. A quick, basic batter that multiplied easily and cooked quickly enough that people wouldn't be waiting forever for their breakfast. Especially not if I started out with a batch of mini-muffins.

I set the oven to preheat and set to work greasing my muffin pans. That done, I started mixing my ingredients, and by the time the oven had heated up, I had my trays of mini-muffins ready to go in the oven. A good thing, too, since Mr. Paul had been the start of a steady stream of customers who kept us busy straight through until the lunchtime rush. By then, I'd at least gotten a few salads and mozzarella-tomato-basil sandwiches ready, although the orders kept coming, and I only ever escaped the kitchen long enough to deliver a freshly made salad or sandwich straight to a customer's table.

I exchanged a few brief words with people I knew and a few more with those who had been at the party. Mary Ellen was cozied up at a small table with her silver fox from the party. He looked slightly less polished than he had when I'd seen him before, but she looked as immaculate as ever.

"Looks like somebody managed to avoid getting sick with the rest of us!" I put Mary Ellen's salad down in front of her and her friend's sandwich in front of him.

Mary Ellen held her hand to her chest and rolled her eyes dramatically. "Don't I wish! I only managed to pull myself out of bed this morning because this handsome man called and just begged me to go to lunch with him!"

"Well, you don't look like it. You look like the picture of health." I grinned at her.

"Makeup, dear," she said, leaning in and putting her hand on my arm. "Very good, very expensive makeup. You can wake up looking like you're ready for death to appear and scoop you up, but with a little dab of this and a little dab of that, you look like nothing worse than tequila has passed between your lips." She gave me a sly wink and smiled.

Mary Ellen always exuded polish and poise, but I could tell she'd turned it up for her friend. She wasn't even trying to hide it either. She had the mysterious ability to pull the curtain back and show men everything behind it, only to have them fall even more in love with her.

I grinned. "I'll have to get you to take me for a makeover sometime."

"Of course, dear. Just say the word."

I thanked her and excused myself back to the kitchen. On the way, I saw Todd and Karli at one of the two-tops along the exposed brick wall and stopped to say hello. Todd had dark circles under his eyes and blond stubble covering his cheeks. Karli, on the other hand, either used the same high-end makeup as Mary Ellen or hadn't drunk any of the poison punch at the party. Of course, I wasn't sure that she'd even had her twentieth birthday yet, so she shouldn't have been anywhere near the alcohol-spiked punch anyway.

I smiled sympathetically at Todd. "How're you doing?"

He raked his hand through his perfectly mussed blond hair. It flopped back down looking even messier but somehow even more perfect. "Been a rough thirty-six hours." He smiled, setting his blue eyes sparkling. He really was excessively good-looking, even in a T-shirt and shorts that had both seen better days.

I turned to Karli, who was dressed in what I took to be her standard uniform of a couple of layered tank tops paired with skintight, not-quite-opaque leggings. Today, the tank tops were neon green and fluorescent yellow, and her eyes were coated in eye shadow to match. "What about you?"

She flicked her thick-lashed eyes at me without turning her head from where it rested on her hand. "I'm fine."

"Karli," Todd said quietly.

She looked at him and turned to me. "I'm fine, really," she repeated, her hot-pink-lacquered lips curling into a smile. "I didn't have any of whatever poisoned everyone."

Todd groaned. Karli shrugged her thin, tanned shoulders. Every time I saw her, I found myself wondering whether that tan came from the sun or a bottle. Of course, this time of year, a tanning bed was likelier than the sun, but I still couldn't tell. She folded a napkin in half then ran the back of her fingernail along the fold, making a tight crease before looking up at Todd. She fluttered her fake lashes at him—not a lot, just enough that I, a former teenage girl, noticed it. "I just want to do whatever I can to help you."

"I know," he said quietly. He reached across the table and patted her hand, letting his linger on hers for just a beat longer than necessary. They'd been seeing each other the summer before, but she'd broken up with him after the murder outside the gym drew her parents' attention to their relationship. At least, that was the story I'd heard from Todd. Now, I wondered if he'd told me the truth—or if things had changed again since then.

They held each other's eyes for long enough that I felt like it was time for me to go. I wished them well and went to step away but backed right into Dean Howard.

He made a big production of stepping back and holding his to-go coffee cup far away from his white dress shirt. "You're lucky you didn't spill any of this on me. This shirt cost more than your whole outfit. It's bad enough that I spent yesterday in front of the toilet because of you."

I bit my tongue to keep myself from snapping back that it was a good thing the dry cleaner was reasonable. It wouldn't have been professional.

Fortunately, Todd stepped in before I had a chance to reconsider. "Give her a break, Dean. It wasn't on purpose. We all feel like crap. We don't have to get on each other's backs about stupid stuff."

"I feel fine," Karli chirped.

Todd shot her a look.

She sank down in her chair, looking visibly chastised.

"Whatever," Dean muttered and escorted himself out.

I watched him go. Then I turned to thank Todd, but Karli already had his attention again. Instead, I slipped away back to the kitchen and the mountain of salads and sandwiches that still needed to be prepared.

Chapter 15

EPHY SHOWED up about halfway through the lunch rush, an hour or two after I would have liked her to be there. I was too busy to stop and check the schedule even though I wanted to, so I just set her to work beside me, having her layer ingredients onto sandwiches and wrap them up to go. As much as I hated to admit it, she was doing a great job— she was fast and efficient, and her sandwiches were beautiful. She even arranged the ingredients so they peeked out tantalizingly from between the slices of bread. I knew my irritation with her wasn't completely justified—my suspicions about the punch were affecting my judgement. I still wanted to check on whether she'd come in on time, though.

Ephy and I emerged from the kitchen when the

lunch rush finally slowed down. We'd managed to get a decent stock of sandwiches and salads ready for the afternoon and could finally go help Sammy out front. Rhonda had come in while we were in the back, so Sammy hadn't been completely alone, but the café still bore the evidence of the busy, hectic lunch service.

"I'm sorry, Fran. It was just so busy. It was all I could do to keep the drinks coming out and—" Sammy started gushing the second she saw me.

"Stop it," Rhonda snapped, somehow still managing to sound affectionate. It was a skill I knew she'd honed over the years of dealing with her two teenaged sons. She waved her hand around the room. "All this means that we were busy. Fran understands if things get a little out of hand while we're busy. Don't you, Fran?" She gave me a look that dared me to say no.

I did understand, but with the piercing glare on Rhonda's face, it would have taken a brave woman to say she didn't. "Of course I do." I took a quick look around the café and realized just why Sammy had jumped to groveling. It looked like a tornado had swept through. A very tame tornado, of course, one that just hovered over the tabletops and scattered plates and cups and napkins and crumbs all around, but a tornado all the same. I was surprised, but given how many salads and sandwiches Ephy and I had churned out, I could guess at the size of the crowd that had rolled through. I smiled at Sammy. "You did great."

Sammy smiled back weakly. She was somehow simultaneously pale and flushed. The edges of her blond hair were matted down with sweat, and her ponytail had slipped down to the nape of her neck. It wasn't just the rush that had her so exhausted—she wasn't fully recovered yet from the ill effects of the poison. "Why don't you head home?" I suggested.

She shook her head, looking anxious, like she thought I was trying to punish her for not having the superhuman power it would have taken to serve everyone and keep the place immaculate too. "No, it's okay. I'll help clean up."

"Sammy, you look like you're going to keel over any second. Go home and take a nap."

"Really, I'm fine."

I sighed. I was as stubborn as they came, but I wasn't sure I was going to win this battle of wills. Not unless I resorted to some underhanded tactics.

"Well, as your boss, I'm telling you it's time for your lunch break. Grab yourself something to eat and go have a seat in the back. We'll see you in half an hour."

I turned away from her before she had a chance to argue. She took a deep breath like she was still going to try then exhaled, grabbed a salad from the case, and disappeared into the back room.

"Well done," Rhonda said quietly to me. "I think she made it through lunch on sheer adrenaline."

"I'm still going to try to get her to go home after her break. She'll run herself ragged if I let her."

Rhonda nodded and grabbed a rag. "Guess I better get to work cleaning things up back here." She started wiping down the counters.

I turned to Ephy, who was examining her cuticles and looked dangerously close to biting one off.

"Ephy, can you work on busing and wiping the tables while I—" I stopped and glanced around the room, trying to figure out where to start. I waved my hand in the air helplessly.

Rhonda chuckled quietly to herself as she scrubbed at a coffee stain on the counter, and Ephy, to her credit, grabbed a dish tub and started clearing dishes from the closest table. I stood for another second and stared, trying to get a grip on the situation. Then I gave up, grabbed another dish tub, and headed to the next table.

We worked slowly but steadily, making our way around the room, clearing dishes from the tables as we went. A few customers came in, and Rhonda stopped her scrubbing to take their orders while I ran and grabbed a clean cloth to wipe off the tables so the customers would have somewhere to sit. I started just following behind Ephy, wiping the tables as she cleared them so at least everything looked a little cleaner. The floor still needed to be swept and mopped, but the sweeping could wait until the dishes were cleared, and the mopping could wait until we closed. At least I kept reminding myself of that to keep from going crazy. I imagined toting around a dustpan and broom under one arm with a mop and bucket under the other while somehow wielding a rag and dish tub at the same time. Even at my overachieving best, I didn't think I could pull that off, so I resigned myself to taking it one step at a time. Slow and steady wins the race and all that.

Slow was the right term for it, but steady wasn't. As customers came in, they naturally sat at the clean tables, which I then had to circle back and clean again. Ephy and I were just getting to the last few tables when Sammy came back into the café from her break.

"I'm going to work on refilling the pastry case," she announced. "Is there anything in particular you want me to focus on, Fran?"

I turned and looked at her with a hand on my hip. She still didn't look too good, although her cheeks weren't as flaming red as they had been before she sat down. "I want you to focus on going home and getting some rest."

"I'm fine, really." But I could see how she was leaning against the counter.

"Then why don't you—"

Before I could finish my sentence, Ephy came in chewing on something. She held a box of chocolates in her hands.

"I found this at the front," Ephy said.

I grabbed the box from her hand. It was a generic box of chocolates, the kind found in the supermarket. My name, "Fran Amaro," was written on a Post-It note that was stuck on top of the box. But just my name. No address, no postmark, no nothing.

I opened the lid and saw a chocolate missing. I turned to Ephy. "You ate one?"

"Why? Do you mind?"

"No, but we don't know who it's from." I frowned, inspecting the box. I hoped it was from Matt. Maybe he'd come by but decided to leave it when he saw how busy we were. My name was written in block letters, which made identifying the writer difficult. He didn't usually write like that, but maybe he was trying to be sneaky.

"Someone left you chocolates?" Rhonda asked, leaning over the counter to look.

"Looks like it." I poked my finger around the edges of the box, looking for a card or anything else that might give me an idea of who had left it or where it had come from, but I found nothing. "Not sure who left it."

"Matt," Rhonda said.

"Probably."

"You're not going to try them?" Ephy looked incredulous. She eyed the box as I put it down on the counter near where she'd found it.

I was surprised. I'd never taken her for the kind of girl to go for chocolates, especially after her comment about not liking sweet stuff. Maybe I needed to talk to Mike about her after all. But her palate had surprised me before, so maybe chocolate just worked for her in a way that other sweets didn't.

"Not right now. I want to get everything cleaned up and the cases restocked before I sit down and have a snack."

Ephy stuck her fingers into the box for another piece before I could stop her. She quickly chewed, and swallowed. Then she coughed—a small, tight little cough.

Her hand went to her chest.

She looked at me with fear in her eyes before crumpling to the floor in a heap.

Chapter 16

I RAN the two steps to her and dropped to the floor by her side. "Ephy!" I yelled. "Ephy!" It had only been a moment since she'd fallen, but she already looked frighteningly lifeless. I didn't think people normally passed out that quickly from choking, but then again, how many people had I ever seen choke?

I struggled to get her limp body into a sitting position so I could give her the Heimlich maneuver, but her torso kept bending over my hands.

"Sammy, call 911!" Rhonda shouted as she ran around the counter and crouched down beside me. Together, we managed to sit Ephy up a little straighter and support her so that we could eject the piece of chocolate from her throat. It wasn't working, though.

Rhonda and I traded places so that I kept Ephy sitting up while Rhonda tried the Heimlich.

Seeing Ephy from this angle made my stomach clench tighter in fear. Ephy's eyes were still open wide, but they had a blank glassiness unlike anything I'd ever seen before. Her skin was even whiter than usual, and her lips had taken on a purple cast. "Harder! Harder!" I yelled at Rhonda.

"I'm trying!" She leaned Ephy forward a little and smacked her hard on the back as though that might jostle the chocolate loose when the proper procedure hadn't. I couldn't blame Rhonda. I was getting tempted to stick my fingers down Ephy's throat to see if I could reach the chocolate and scrape it out. I might have tried that out of sheer desperation if professional help hadn't arrived just then.

Ryan Leary, officer in the Cape Bay Police Department and Sammy's boyfriend, ran through the door and came straight to where Rhonda and I were crouched down with Ephy. "Lay her down flat."

"She choked on a piece of chocolate," I said as he grabbed her wrist in his right hand. After a moment, he dropped her wrist and grabbed the other one. He frowned, adjusted his grip, and waited again. He shook his head and looked at me and Rhonda. "Do either of you know CPR?"

"Sort of," I said, trying to remember the details of what I'd learned in the CPR class I'd taken back in high school.

Fortunately, Rhonda's skills were fresher than mine. "I'm certified."

"You do breaths and count. I'll do compressions." Ryan said something into the radio perched on his shoulder as they both moved into position. "Ready?" Rhonda nodded. He looked at his watch. "Okay, let's go." Ryan started pumping Ephy's chest as Rhonda counted along. When she got to thirty, Ryan stopped, and Rhonda bent to breathe twice into Ephy's mouth. Even I could see her chest rise and fall with the two breaths. If air was getting through to her lungs, that meant she hadn't choked after all.

Ryan and Rhonda were only a few rounds into their CPR when the paramedics arrived. Ryan rattled off a bunch of words that I took to mean something about Ephy's condition as he and Rhonda stepped back to make room for the paramedics to take over for them.

It was the second time in only a few months that I'd witnessed a scene like this, but it was no easier than it had been the first time. If anything, it was more upsetting this time around.

As the paramedics did their work, Ryan guided Rhonda, Sammy, and me toward the back of the café. By some miracle, we'd been completely empty of customers when Ephy collapsed, so it was just the three of us and Ryan. "Mike's on his way," he said. "He'll want to talk to you."

I wasn't sure whether he meant just me or all three of us, but we nodded.

Ryan looked towards the door apprehensively. He shifted his feet and rubbed his hands together. Sammy got up and put her arms around him. He hugged her back. I suddenly found myself desperately wishing Matt were there.

Rhonda grabbed my hand and squeezed it. I squeezed back. If Matt wasn't there, at least my friends were.

A blur of a man sprinted past the front windows and burst through the door. Mike looked at the body on the floor and the paramedics around it for a long few seconds then over at us. His eyes closed as he exhaled. He pressed his lips together then, after another moment, opened them again and became all business.

Mike strode over to one of the paramedics who was standing to the side, talking on his radio. They spoke briefly in low tones that I couldn't hear. Mike nodded a few times and then came over to us. I thought he would be as hard, brusque, and businesslike as ever, but something else was in his eyes as he walked over. He looked at each of our faces before he said anything, and then it was the last thing I would have expected.

"I'm glad you're all safe." He looked from one of our faces to the next again, nodded, and pulled his notebook out of his pocket. He opened it with a flick of his wrist and clicked the end of his pen. "What do we know, Leary?"

"Arrived on scene to find a female, early twenties, lying on the floor unconscious and unresponsive with no pulse. Fran and Rhonda were attempting the Heimlich maneuver. I—"

"Wait," Mike interrupted. "The Heimlich? Why?" He looked at me with an expression that wasn't quite as judgmental as I expected but also not as sympathetic as I would have liked.

"We thought she was choking," I said, as if that weren't obvious.

It must have not been obvious to him because he looked exasperated as he repeated, "*Why?*"

"She ate one of those chocolates over there right before she collapsed." I moved to go get the box to show him, but he put his arm out and stopped me.

"No, don't touch it." He walked over there. "Leary, get this all bagged up. We need it finger-printed and tested for... everything."

Ryan nodded and headed for the door. Mike turned back to us. "So where did these chocolates come from?"

I shook my head and shrugged. "Someone left them while we were busy."

"Someone? Who? Approximately what time?"

I turned my hands palms up and looked at Rhonda and Sammy. They didn't know any more than we did. "I don't know. Sometime between nine and two is the best I can tell you on time."

He sighed with barely concealed frustration. I knew better than to take it personally.

Another ambulance pulled up outside. The two paramedics who jumped out of the cab went around to the back and brought out a gurney. We watched them load Ephy onto it and roll her out to the ambulance, still trying to bring her back to life. As quickly as they'd arrived, they were gone.

Mike went over to talk to the guy who appeared to be in charge while the couple of guys who were left picked up their gear. They exchanged a lot of nods and "uh-huhs," and then the paramedics left.

Ryan came in with a pair of gloves and a handful of evidence bags. He and Mike spoke quietly, then Ryan snapped on the gloves and started carefully putting the box of chocolates into the bags. Mike walked back over to us, looking subdued. "She have any allergies?" He jerked his head in the direction they'd taken Ephy.

I could only shrug. "She never mentioned anything. Does that mean you think she had an allergic reaction?" I felt hope rise in my chest. If it was an allergic reaction, they could give her drugs and she'd be back on her feet in no time.

Mike closed his notebook and put it back in his pocket, ignoring my question. "Look, I don't have any reason why you can't get back to work, but don't go eating any food if you don't know where it came from, okay? I'll be in touch." He headed for the door and waited while Ryan gave Sammy a quick hug goodbye.

They left, and I turned to look at Sammy and Rhonda.

Sammy had sat down at one of the tables and was holding her head in her hands. She looked paler than ever.

Rhonda had her arms crossed tightly across her chest. Her face was pinched and looked anxious.

There was no way we could open back up.

I dropped down into a chair. "You guys can go home. I can't sit here and smile and serve people coffee this afternoon not knowing how Ephy is."

Rhonda gave me a look. "Fran, I think Ephy—I don't think—" She stopped and blinked rapidly, looking like she was in pain.

"Don't." I put my hand up in a signal to stop. "They were still working on her when they left. We don't know anything."

Rhonda nodded.

"I don't want to go home," Sammy said. "I don't want to sit there alone and think about—" She waved her hand toward the area where Ephy had fallen. Her blue eyes filled up with tears.

I was at a loss. I didn't really want to be alone, either, but I knew I couldn't function well enough to work. Matt would still be at the office, but at least I'd have Latte.

Rhonda clapped her hands together. "Let's go out and get something to eat."

"Are you serious?"

"What did your mother always do when you had a bad day at school?"

The sudden change of subject threw me for a loop, and I didn't know how to answer.

"She sat you down and fed you," Rhonda said in her best mom-like tone of voice. "So let's go get something to eat. It'll take our mind off what happened, and we can talk. Now go get your purses, both of you."

I didn't think either Sammy or I knew what else to do or had the emotional energy to argue, so we did as we were told and got our purses then headed out the door.

I shuddered as I locked it behind me. People kept getting sick in my café, and it terrified me.

Chapter 17

WE ENDED up sitting on the deck at a restaurant that had just opened up a couple of weeks before. It was the kind of place that came and went in a beachside town—open for a year or two then shuttered again when the owners realized that they hadn't made enough from the tourist season to pay the rent through the winter. Some businesses made it, of course—mine was one of them—but they were more the exception than the rule.

The restaurant we were sitting in was the third that had been in the building in the last ten years. It was a great location with a beautiful view that had tourists flocking to it during the season, but the same thing that made it successful was also what led to the restaurants' downfall. Restauranteurs fell in love with the location and all the money they made from the tourists but forgot that we locals weren't going anywhere just for a view we saw every day and that rent still had to be paid in the winter.

In any case, the drinks and appetizers were good. Not that we were enjoying them much. It was hard to have an appetite when you'd just seen what we had.

"She'll be okay, won't she?" Sammy asked, staring at the iced tea in front of her. She always had an aura of sweet innocence about her, but this sounded naïve even for her.

Rhonda looked at me. I looked at the lobster lettuce wrap in front of me. I couldn't get the sight of Ephy's blue lips out of my mind. Even after all that CPR, she was still limp and blue when they carried her out.

"Sammy, I don't—" Rhonda started.

Sammy cut her off with an imploring look. "Just say yes."

Rhonda met her eye and then looked down. "I really hope so."

"How is everything?" Our chirpy waitress had appeared beside us as we all stared at the table. "Everything tasting delicious?"

I looked up at her, wondering how to explain

that our plates were all untouched. As much as I was now worried about people eating the food at my café, I usually worried when they didn't.

Her cheery smile faltered slightly when she finally seemed to notice that none of us were eating. "Did I get your order wrong or something? It looks like you haven't touched a thing!" She pulled out her notepad and started looking at what she'd jotted down.

For some reason, I still couldn't find the words to string together to explain that everything was right—we just weren't in the mood to eat it.

She looked up from her notepad with her lips pressed together as she scanned the table again. "Well, it looks like——"

"Our friend just collapsed in front of us and had to get rushed to the hospital in an ambulance," Rhonda said brusquely. "We're just taking a minute to talk about that." *Leave it to Rhonda to take the situation in hand*, I thought.

"Oh, um, okay. Um——" The waitress's eyes scanned the table like she was trying to remember if there had been a fourth member of our party when we sat down, and she'd just somehow missed the ambulance carting her off.

"We'll call you if need you," Rhonda said. Even

with her tendency to be blunt, she sounded a little cold.

The waitress, still looking confused, glanced around the table again, then turned on her heel and walked away.

"It's not her fault. She didn't know," Sammy said quietly.

Rhonda looked at me.

I gave a half-hearted shrug. "You did come across a little harsh."

She sighed and wiped at the condensation on her water glass. "I'll leave her a good tip."

We sat in silence for a few long minutes before Rhonda picked up her fork and stabbed her lobster salad. "What?" she asked when Sammy and I looked at her. "I'm paying for it. I may as well eat it. It doesn't do Ephy any good to let it go to waste."

She wasn't wrong, but that didn't make me feel any more like eating. Sammy did start to poke at her fried clams, though. I wasn't even sure why I had ordered anything when my head was swirling so fast that I could barely put my worries into words.

"Do you think it's something about the café?"

Rhonda made a face around her mouthful of lobster salad.

"What could it be?" Sammy asked, rolling a clam over with her fork. She still hadn't gotten any of them to her mouth, instead playing with them and moving them around the way a child did when they were hoping to convince their mom that they were eating when they really weren't. "We're all fine."

"This time," Rhonda said, having swallowed.

Sammy looked stricken.

"This time, yes," I agreed. "But who knows why? Maybe Ephy is just more susceptible to whatever's going on, and that's why she—"

I cut myself off, seeing her limp body again in my mind's eye. She was just a kid. Becky and Amanda leapt to my mind. What if something happened to them? I would never forgive myself. Ephy was in her early twenties—young enough to still seem like a kid—but Becky and Amanda really were kids. Kids whose parents lived in town and came into my coffee shop on a regular basis. For their own safety, I'd have to take them off the schedule until whatever was happening was sorted out. Rhonda, Sammy, and I would just have to hold down the fort. But Rhonda had a family. I put my head in my hands. It was too much.

Sammy put her hand on my back and rubbed it gently. "It's okay, Fran."

"It's not," I moaned.

"It will be."

I dragged my hands down my face and looked at Rhonda for some commiseration. She looked alarmingly sympathetic, which just made me feel worse.

"Dwelling on it isn't going to help, Fran," she said quietly. "Even if it is something about the café, there's nothing we can do about it until we know what it is. The hospital will do an aut—" She stopped and looked at Sammy's wide eyes. "The hospital will do tests to find out why Ephy collapsed. For all we know, she choked."

"She didn't choke," I interjected. "I've seen people choke." I didn't add that if she had choked, I didn't have high hopes for her after the amount of time she'd been down and how much CPR she'd had.

Rhonda gave me a look I could imagine her using on her kids and continued. "For all we know," she repeated emphatically, "she choked. Until the hospital takes a look at her, we don't know anything. Now eat your lettuce wraps before you get loopy from low blood sugar."

I looked helplessly down at the plate in front of me. The suggestion that Ephy choked to death didn't make me any more inclined to put something in my mouth.

"It will make you feel better."

"It will make me feel nauseous," I said. "More nauseous. I already feel nauseous."

"We all do. But we're going to eat our food because someone cooked it for us and if we're going to figure out why people are getting sick at the café, we need our bodies to be strong." She looked at Sammy. "What was it her mom used to say?" She didn't wait for an answer. "*Food feeds the heart and nourishes the soul.* Your heart and soul need nourishment. You need to eat. Your mother would want you to."

It was a low blow. We were coming up on the one-year anniversary of my mom's sudden death, and Rhonda knew I still got emotional about it. Even now, I felt the tears burning in my eyes.

"She's right, Fran," Sammy said softly. "The first thing your mom would do whenever somebody came in upset about something was to have sit them down and make them eat."

I knew they were right, but I wasn't ready to admit it.

"Do you remember last fall when Amanda came in crying because she failed her chorus final?" Sammy asked Rhonda.

Rhonda smiled at the memory. "She prepared the wrong song, didn't she?"

Sammy nodded. "Your mom let her clock in and then had her go sit down at a table. Amanda thought she was in trouble or something, but then your mom came out with a basil-tomato-mozzarella sandwich and a bowl of minestrone and sat across from her until Amanda ate every last bite. And then she told Amanda about the time she made a tarte instead of a torte for an exam in culinary school."

A reluctant smile spread across my face. I'd heard that story before too. And I'd been force-fed soup on more than one occasion growing up when I was anxious about a test or sad about a boy. It really did help. I just wished my mother was here to force-feed me soup now.

"Your mom's not here to make you eat now, but I am," Rhonda said, as if she could read my mind.

I nodded. Nodding was all I could manage with the tears that threatened to fall.

"Did you hear the one about the guy who walked into a bar?"

I looked at Rhonda in confusion.

"You look like you need a joke." She looked over at Sammy. "I think we all need a joke. So did you hear the one about the guy who walked into a bar?" She waited a moment and then delivered the punchline. "It hurt."

I laughed despite myself at the sheer stupidity of the joke.

"What do you call a fish with no eyes?" Sammy asked. "A fsh."

I laughed again. A couple of tears squeezed out of my eyes, but the dumb jokes had worked. I wiped the tears away with my napkin.

"Why was six afraid of seven?" Rhonda said. "Because seven eight nine. Get it? Seven *ate* nine?"

I rolled my eyes but giggled.

"Now eat, Fran!"

"Okay, okay." I held my hands up in surrender. I still didn't think I could stomach anything, but I knew when I was defeated. Rhonda wasn't going to let me leave the table until I ate, and if I was honest with myself, my mother wouldn't have let me either.

I looked down at the lettuce wraps that under other circumstances would look appealing and took a deep breath. I had just convinced myself that maybe I could get a few bites down when the door from the restaurant to the deck swung open, and Mike strode through.

He looked tired and worn. It had only been a little over an hour since I'd seen him last, but he seemed to have aged five years. His hair was rumpled, and he had dark circles under his eyes.

He scanned the room and landed on me. "We need to talk." He nodded to a table at the opposite corner of the patio.

I had to admit I was grateful to have an excuse to leave my plate. I may have been used to swallowing down food every time I was feeling down, but that didn't mean I was excited to do it. With a quick look at Sammy and Rhonda, I followed Mike to the far corner. He took the chair against the wall where he could see the door, and I sat across from him.

He leaned back in his chair, closed his eyes, and took a deep breath. I could tell that he had bad news.

After a moment, he rubbed his face with his hands then ran them through his hair. "Tell me again about the box of chocolates."

I wanted to ask about Ephy, but I wasn't ready to have my suspicions about her death confirmed. I shrugged. "I already told you everything I know."

He gave me a look that seemed like he wanted to be annoyed but was too tired. "Tell me again."

I sighed and started in. "We were really busy during lunch. While we were cleaning up, Ephy found the box of chocolates and brought it in."

Mike pulled a notebook out of his pocket and started scribbling. "Did you see the box before Ephy found it?"

"No."

"Where was it?"

"On the counter, I guess. Ephy was—"

"On the counter, you guess?" Mike repeated, sounding skeptical.

I bit my tongue to keep from snapping at him, but I was less successful at keeping the exasperation out of my voice. "I don't know, Mike. I didn't see it, remember?"

He looked at me with one eyebrow raised, but, to his credit, looked right back down at his notepad. "What about Sammy and Rhonda?"

"I don't think so. They would have said something."

"I'll have to talk to them."

I turned around to call them over, but he stopped me.

"Later. Who was in the café today?"

"Are you serious?" I asked.

"Mm-hmm." He didn't even look up.

"I have no idea. I was working. And we were busy."

His eyebrow went up as he tapped his pen on the notepad.

"I could give you some names, but it won't be nearly everyone. And I didn't know everyone who was in. It's not the full season yet, but we're starting to get tourist traffic—"

"I'll need to see your credit card receipts."

I nodded. "Not a problem." I didn't bother pointing out that lots of people still paid cash, particularly regulars who had a usual and knew their total off the tops of their heads. A little voice in the back of my mind reminded me that those regulars were the people most likely to have been at the party, but I didn't want to think about that now —or ever.

He ran through a few more questions about whether anyone saw the package get delivered, how it was wrapped, and who had touched it. Then he leaned back again in the chair. "The chocolates and the box are on their way to the state lab for testing. They have more resources up there than we do, and I don't want to miss anything." He stopped and shook his head. "I don't like this, Fran."

I wanted to snap back that he should try it from my side for a while, but I controlled myself. "You said the chocolates are on their way to the lab. That means she didn't—"

His sad eyes met mine. "She didn't choke."

I knew what he was going to say next but willed him to say something else.

"The doctor said it didn't fit the pattern of an allergic reaction either. We think the chocolates were poisoned. I'm sorry, Franny, but the indications are that she was gone before she hit the floor."

I clapped my hand over my mouth as I tried to gulp back a sob. It was the result I had known was coming, but it still felt like a gut punch. Poor Ephy. All she'd wanted was some chocolate. I couldn't hold myself back anymore and burst into sobs. I heard Sammy and Rhonda's chairs being pushed back, and then their arms were around me, their own tears mingling with mine.

"She's gone?" Rhonda asked.

"I'm sorry," Mike answered quietly. "Did she have an emergency contact on file?"

"It would be with her employment paperwork," Rhonda answered for me.

"I'll come by and get it later. They're starting the autopsy soon, and I want to be there for it. I'll call you later, Franny."

I nodded, still sobbing.

He got up to leave but stopped and put his hand on my shoulder first. "I'm so sorry." His heavy footsteps crossed the patio and faded away as the three of us sat in the corner and cried.

Chapter 18

HOURS LATER, I was curled up on the couch with Latte, the TV playing a repeat of a baking competition I'd seen at least a dozen times but at least found comforting and familiar. Matt was banging around in the kitchen, making an awful racket. He'd said he was going to make us dinner, but it didn't sound like it was going very well so far. He only knew how to make two things, one of which was spaghetti with meat sauce, so I didn't know how wrong it could go, but I wasn't optimistic based on the muttering I was hearing.

I buried my face in Latte's fur and inhaled. He probably needed a bath, but his dog smell was comforting. I scratched his head, and he twisted around to lick my face.

A quiet knock came at the door. Latte picked his head up, ready to run to the door and defend our abode and all that lived in it, but then put his head back down against my arm, deciding snuggles were more important than defense.

The knock came again, a little bit louder this time.

"Matt!"

"Yeah?" he called from the kitchen.

"Could you get the door and tell whoever it is to go away?"

"Someone's at the door?"

I cuddled a little closer to Latte.

Matt came out of the kitchen, drying his hands on a dishtowel, his sweatshirt half-soaked. "You said someone's at the door?"

"Yes," I mumbled. "Tell them to go away."

He shrugged and went to open the door. "Hey, man!" he said cheerfully. "Franny said to go away."

"I wouldn't want you to let me in either."

Matt chuckled and swung the door open wide. "Come on in."

I didn't get up. I'd known that it was Mike the second I'd heard Matt's greeting. I liked Mike, but I didn't feel the need to get up and make him feel welcome, especially not today, not when I knew he was here to grill me more.

"Have a seat," Matt said, welcoming Mike into my house. "You want a beer?"

"I'm on duty."

"Some water, then?"

"Sure." Mike sat down on the chair closest to my head while Matt went and got him a glass of water.

I heard the clinking of the glass and then the water running from the faucet, then Matt reappeared. "Here you go. Can I get you anything else?" When Mike shook his head, Matt looked between us and then started backing towards the kitchen. "I'm supposed to be making dinner, so I'll just leave you guys alone to chat, then."

I didn't appreciate the assumption that Mike was here to talk to me or that it was private or that it was okay to have let him inside in the first place. I didn't doubt that he was correct, but I didn't like it either.

"You can stay, Matt," Mike said. "Franny'd probably appreciate it."

Matt shrugged and sat down at the far end of the couch, pulling my feet onto his lap. I noticed that he didn't protest too vigorously about getting back to his meal prep.

"How're you doing, Franny?" Mike asked after a few seconds.

"How do I look?" I asked, not bothering to sound or act any more cheerful than I felt.

"About like I expected."

I scratched Latte some more, and he rewarded me with more kisses.

"We need to get in touch with Ephy's next of kin. You have an emergency contact for her?"

"It's at the café."

He nodded and took a deep breath. "I want to search the café again, so if it's okay with you, I'll just get it while I'm there."

"That's fine," I mumbled into Latte's fur.

"Wait, why do you want to search the café again?" Matt asked. "You think something has changed since yesterday?"

"Due diligence. Whoever left the chocolates may have dropped something."

"Like their driver's license?"

"I can only hope," Mike said. "So that's fine with you, Franny?"

I nodded.

"Don't you need a warrant to search it?" Matt asked.

"If the owner doesn't give me permission to search, which is her right." Mike looked at me. "I don't want you to feel like I'm pressuring you or anything. There's nothing wrong with saying no." He hesitated. "It means I'll have go to the judge and plead my case, but that's a part of the job. No hard feelings if you decline."

Matt looked at me expectantly. I could tell he wanted me to tell Mike to get the warrant, but I didn't care. I just wanted it to be over. "Search it. Please. Ephy died on my watch, eating chocolates that were for me. I want whoever did it to be caught. If you have to search the café every day for the next year to catch them, then do it."

"Thank you, Fran." Mike and Matt exchanged a look that I didn't care to decode. They'd been friends a long time. Whatever it was, they'd be fine. "While I'm here, there's something else I want to talk to you about." He fidgeted in his chair. "The first attack was at your birthday party, and over a hundred people were poisoned. The second attack was at your café and killed a person. The chocolates used in the second attack were addressed to you.

Fran, I don't think we can avoid the fact that you are the target."

I couldn't say that the thought hadn't been vaguely in the back of my mind, but to hear him state it so clearly sent a chill down my spine. And Matt's, apparently, based on the way he gripped my foot.

"I'd like you to lay low for a while. Stay home. Keep the café closed."

"What?" I sat up for the first time. Latte wasn't pleased and jumped off the couch then wandered into the kitchen to look for any errant food scraps. "I can't stay at home. I can't close the café. People depend on us. They count on us for their morning coffee. My employees depend on their paychecks. I have—"

"Exactly, Fran." Mike leaned forward and looked me dead in the eye. I suddenly realized how intimidating he must be to the people he was investigating. "People depend on you. They love you, and they love your coffee. And your employees depend on their jobs. That's why you can't go running around endangering your life. You're not being selfish by closing the café. You're being selfish if you open it. Ephy's dead, Fran. I don't want to be investigating your death next."

I sat back on the couch as Matt leaned forward. "Come on, Mike, don't be so hard on her."

Mike fixed that dark glare on Matt. "You may not like my tone, but tell me you wouldn't feel better knowing she was safe at home instead of out interacting with the public when we know for a fact that someone is trying to kill her."

Matt sat in stunned silence. Mike looked from one of us to the other. "I'm sorry if I'm coming off a little harsh, but this is serious, Fran. Whatever was in those chocolates killed Ephy, and the box had your name on it."

I nodded silently. He was right. Someone had tried to kill me, and an innocent bystander had died in my place. It wasn't safe to go back to the café. "Okay. I'll call the girls and let them know we'll be closed for a few days."

"It may be longer than a few days," Mike said.

I nodded. Whatever he said. Whatever it took to keep everyone safe.

Mike opened his mouth to speak, but his cell phone rang. He pulled it out of his pocket and looked at the display. "I have to take this," he said, and he stepped into the kitchen.

Matt reached over and pulled me against him. I leaned into his chest, breathing in his smell and the comfort of his arms. I couldn't quite wrap my head around the situation I found myself in. Someone was trying to kill me—and not just a spur-of-the-moment thing, like when I'd been pushed down a flight of stairs. Someone was actively, premeditatedly trying to kill me. Why would anyone want me dead? What had I done to anyone to make them hate me that much?

The low sound of Mike's phone call ended, and he reappeared in the living room. "State lab. They have the preliminary results on the chocolates. No fingerprints, but the chocolates appear to have been injected through the bottom with large quantities of pure nicotine, easily enough to kill. The holes on the bottom were covered up with a smear of chocolate. Easy enough to notice if you look at the bottom, but why would you do that?"

"Oh God." I buried my face in Matt's chest. I should have told Ephy to poke the bottom. I should have told her to at least look. She could still be alive if we'd just looked at the bottoms of the chocolates.

"It wasn't your fault, Franny," Mike said quietly.

Matt rubbed my back, murmuring softly in my ear that it was going to be okay and that it wasn't my fault. But it was. I knew it was. Maybe he didn't think so, but I knew it was.

"I'm, uh, I'm gonna get out of here. I'm gonna head over to the café to start the search if that's still okay."

I was crying, but I felt Matt nod against my head.

"I'll give you guys a call if I have any trouble finding Ephy's emergency contact."

Matt nodded again.

There was a pause and then, for the second time that day, Mike crossed the room and left while I sobbed.

Chapter 19

I HAD the curtains drawn and all the lights off when Matt got to my house sometime around noon the next day. He had gone in to work that morning but only after Mike's assurances that the attacks had all been fairly passive—food or drinks left for me or someone else to consume at our leisure. There was no reason to think I wasn't safe alone in my house. So he had gone in, but he promised me he'd take a long lunch and come back to the house to check on me.

"Franny?" he called from the doorway.

"In here." I was in virtually the same position on the couch that I'd been the night before—curled up with Latte, staring mindlessly at bakers on the TV screen.

Matt stood in the entry for a moment, looking at me, before walking over to the window. "Let's get some light in here," he said, jerking the curtains open.

"Don't!" I covered my eyes with my forearm. The light from outside was blinding.

"You'll get used to it in a minute." He moved over to the other window.

"No, really, please don't."

He turned and looked at me with his brow furrowed. "Why not?"

"I just—" I shook my head. "I don't want them open."

Slowly, Matt closed both the curtains. "I could turn the lights on?" he asked, moving over to the switch.

I shook my head. "No, I want it like it is."

He came over to where I was sitting on the couch, sat down beside me, and pulled me close. "What's going on, Franny?"

I pulled away and turned so I could look at him. "What's going on? Someone's trying to kill me, remember?"

"Yeah, but Mike said—"

"I don't care what Mike said. He's not the one being chased down by a crazed murderer."

"In fairness, whoever it is isn't exactly trying to chase you down."

"No, they're just trying to poison me." I glared at him. "What happened to you being worried about my safety? Yesterday, when Mike was here, you were all for me closing the café and staying at home, but now all of a sudden you want to act like everything's normal."

Latte jumped down off the couch and slunk away. He wasn't used to me raising my voice about anything other than the occasional yelp when I burned myself in the kitchen—or the odd occasion when he got a little too close to something dead on one of our walks.

"Franny, I—" He reached out to take my hand, but I pulled it away. "Of course I'm concerned about your safety. I just don't think it's healthy for you to be afraid of opening the curtains."

"I don't think poison is healthy."

Matt looked at me for a long moment before pulling me close again. This time I let him.

"I'm scared, Matty," I whispered after a few minutes. "I'm scared of what might happen to me, to you, to Latte, to Sammy and Rhonda. I'm just really scared."

"I know." He stroked my hair and brushed his

lips across the top of my head. "I know. I'm scared, too, but I would never leave you if I didn't trust Mike's judgement and trust that you were safe here."

I nodded my head against his chest.

"I love you, Franny."

"I love you, too," I murmured.

Matt held me for a few minutes until his stomach grumbled—loudly. Latte lifted his head and tilted it back and forth, trying to figure out what the noise was and where it came from. Despite myself, I giggled. And then Matt chuckled. He looked down at me with a warmth and softness that made me wonder why I'd ever been afraid when I knew he would do anything to protect me.

"Want me to reheat the rest of the pizza for lunch?" he asked. After Mike had left the night before, Matt admitted that he hadn't gotten any further than knocking half the pots out of the cabinet and splashing water everywhere when he dropped the pot he was filling up for spaghetti. We ordered a pizza instead.

I nodded. "Yes, please."

He kissed me softly before getting up. "Is it okay if I turn some lights on so I can see what I'm doing?"

Remembering the disaster he'd made of my kitchen the night before, I agreed. Twenty or so minutes later, he was back next to me on the couch, lights on, eating our leftover slices. It wasn't the best pizza—you're not really setting yourself up for success in that regard when you order at nine o'clock at night—but it had been edible, and it reheated well, so I was happy. It also helped that that pizza was the first thing I'd eaten all day. In fact, Matt ended up handing over his last slice after I inhaled everything on mine and he caught me eyeing his plate.

When we were finished eating, he sat and watched until the end of the current episode of the baking competition with me. He even tolerated my commentary as I yelled at the bakers to put their dough in the freezer instead of the refriger-ator and then to get it out of the freezer before it froze solid.

"You should apply for one of these," he said at one point, a sly smile spreading across his face. "Since you know everything they should be doing."

"Oh, like you should apply to play for the Patri-ots? You seem to be forgetting that I hear you yelling at the TV during football season... and basketball season... and hockey season."

"Point taken," he said, but the twinkle didn't leave his eyes.

When the show was over, he patted me on the knee. "I better be getting back to work." He gave me a tender look. "You going to be okay here on your own?"

I nodded. "I have Latte. He'll protect me."

Matt looked down at Latte, who was currently asleep on his back in the middle of the floor, his paws in the air, looking like he wouldn't harm a fly, let alone an intruder. "Vicious mutt."

"His DNA test said he's a purebred."

"Vicious purebred." Matt grinned at me. "I'm glad you've perked up. I was worried about you—" He held up his hand to keep me from cutting him off. "And not just because someone tried to poison you. The Franny I know and love doesn't give up and sit in the dark when things go wrong." He paused and chuckled. "The Franny who annoys the crap out of Mike doesn't either. Before you get any ideas, I'm not saying you should leave the house and go investigate or anything, just that you're always saying you don't have enough time to do the things you want—like experiment with new recipes, or move into the downstairs bedroom."

He was right. The café kept me too busy to

really experiment in the kitchen the way I would have liked to—everything from new drinks to new baked goods took time for me to figure out, time I didn't usually have. And I'd been trying to move into the downstairs bedroom practically since I moved back into my childhood home. Maybe spending a few days at home wasn't such a bad thing after all.

"Okay, you're right," I conceded and quickly made a face at his expression of faux shock. "I'll try to find something productive to do this afternoon."

He moved in and gave me a goodbye kiss then started backing towards the door. "Just don't watch the next episode without me," he said, gesturing at the TV.

"I've seen it three times already."

He gave me a dirty look. "Just for that, I'm not making you my trademark spaghetti Bolognese tonight."

"You mean destroying my kitchen?" I teased.

He rolled his eyes. "I'll see you tonight." He left, and I stared at the TV, trying to decide how to spend my time. Spending my day—or days—at home was just giving in to whoever had it in for me, and I wasn't the type who gave in.

"What should I do, Latte?"

He rolled onto his side but didn't wake up.

"A lot of help you are."

I wandered into the kitchen. Some coffee would help get me going. Some coffee was my standard solution for almost everything. I briefly considered playing with a new recipe using my home espresso machine, but I quickly decided that I'd rather stick with a classic latte. I did take the time—as always—to create a little latte art, pouring in a picture of a phoenix to inspire me.

When the coffee was ready, I went back out to the living room. Latte had taken advantage of my absence and moved back on the couch, sprawled out on top of my blanket. I wedged myself in and tried to think of what to do next. When it finally occurred to me—sometime shortly after the caffeine hit my bloodstream—it was so obvious I didn't know how I hadn't thought of it sooner. I had the list of people who'd been at the party, and I'd been working at the café yesterday. I could easily compare the list to who I'd seen the day before to figure out who had the opportunity to commit both poisonings.

Matt and Mike couldn't possibly begrudge me a little detective work while I was holed up in my house, could they?

Chapter 20

AN HOUR LATER, I had a complete list of everyone I could think of who had been at the party and at the café the day Ephy was poisoned. I was sure I didn't have everyone, though. I picked up my phone and dialed Sammy.

When she answered, I could hear kitchen sounds in the background.

"Hi, Sammy. Do you have a few minutes to talk? It sounds like you're busy."

"Sure," she chirped. "I was just starting dinner. Ryan and I are both off tonight, and I actually have time to cook, so I decided to make something nice."

We chatted for a few minutes about the roast chicken she was making before I managed to turn the conversation around to the party guests who had been at the café the day before.

"Are you trying to investigate the poisonings yourself?" she asked immediately.

"I'm just trying to think of who had opportunity, that's all," I replied.

"I don't know, Fran. You know Mike doesn't like you getting involved in his investigations."

"I'm not getting involved," I tried to assure her. "I'm just thinking about it. I'll tell Mike anyone we come up with."

Sammy still hesitated. I could hear faint sizzling through the line as she started her gravy base. "You are going to tell him, right? You're not going to go confront anyone yourself?"

"No, I'm just trying to get a list together."

Another pause. "Don't you think the police have thought of that already? Ryan said that this case is killing Mike."

"Gosh, I hope not."

"You know what I mean, Fran!"

I did. But I also knew that I was the one whose life was actually in danger.

"I'm sorry for being flippant," I said, genuine contrition in my voice. "It's just driving me crazy sitting here at home with nothing to do."

"You said you wanted to add some new drinks to the menu for the summer season. You could work on that. You always come up with really creative stuff."

"Have you been talking to Matt?"

Sammy giggled. "No, did he say the same thing?"

"Yes," I groaned. "I know I could work on that, but I want to feel like I'm doing something useful. Like I'm not just sitting here waiting for the poisoner to figure out what they're doing and actually kill me."

I could feel Sammy's stillness through the phone line. "I'm so sorry, Fran," she said in a small voice. "You're right. Who do you have on your list so far?"

I rattled off a handful of names, including Mary Ellen and her beau, Todd Caruthers, and Dean Howard.

"Mr. Paul was at the party, and I remember he came in early yesterday."

"Mr. Paul?" I asked.

"That's just what I call him to be polite. It's Paul. I'm not sure of his last name. I think he's a lawyer or something over in Barnstable. He comes in early every day."

I vaguely remembered him being the first

customer through the door the day before. I wrote his name down, even though "Paul something who might be a lawyer" wasn't the most helpful information. As far as I was concerned, it was better to include too many names than to leave off an important one. Besides, even if I didn't know this Paul guy, maybe he knew me. I shivered. The thought of someone I didn't even know wanting me dead was even more chilling than someone I did know wanting me dead. "Anyone else?"

"Ummm…" Sammy thought for a minute. "I don't think so. Oh! Melissa. Melissa was in."

"Really? I don't remember seeing her."

"Yeah, she was in for just a minute. She bought some cookies for her office."

I jotted down Melissa's name. I didn't think she was capable of hurting a soul, even when not heavily pregnant, but if I was putting Paul on the list, I needed to put Melissa down too.

Sammy couldn't think of anyone else, but she promised that she'd call me back if she did. I wished her luck on her chicken then said goodbye.

Rhonda was next on my list.

"Hey, Fran!" she answered. "Stop it! You're being rude!"

I sat in silence, wondering what I'd said or done

to merit that greeting. Then I heard the distant but distinct sounds of gas being passed, accompanied by vigorous burping.

"Not you, Fran. I have the boys in the car and —stop it!—they're having an armpit fart competition. And burping, just for good measure. You two are disgusting! You're on speaker, by the way. We're in the car."

"I caught that," I said, determining that the last bit was for me. "Should I call you back later?"

"No. No! No! Stop it! Get out! Go! Get out! Stop it, you're disgusting, get out! You're fine, Fran, go ahead."

"Um—" I hesitated, not sure I wanted to be part of Rhonda abandoning her teenage sons on the side of the road.

"It's fine. We got to the soccer field. I have some peace for an hour or so."

"Are you sure?" I asked. "You don't need to go watch them or anything?"

"It's just practice," Rhonda said. "I've seen enough hours of soccer practice for my lifetime and yours. What's up?"

Hoping to avoid the grilling I'd gotten from Sammy, I gave Rhonda a vague explanation of what I wanted to know—just that I was trying to remember which regulars we had at the café yesterday afternoon. She knew me too well, though.

"You're trying to figure out who the poisoner is, aren't you?" she said immediately.

The long silence while I tried to come up with a plausible denial gave me away.

"Don't worry, I won't tell Mike a thing. His kids practice at a different time anyway," Rhonda said with a chuckle. "So, who do you have so far?"

I rattled off the names on my list, including the two Sammy gave me.

"Mrs. D'Angelo," Rhonda said immediately.

I went to write her name down then stopped. "Wait, was she?" I didn't remember seeing her on either occasion. I wondered how I'd missed her.

"Oh, yes. She cornered me both times. I think I still have talon marks."

Mrs. D'Angelo was known for, among other things, her lengthy fingernails, always perfectly manicured in blood red, which she frequently used to grasp her unwilling conversation victims. "Conversation," of course, was a generous term for what was really a monologue on Mrs. D'Angelo's part.

"She didn't get sick at the party, did she?" As

annoying as the older woman could be, I hoped she hadn't been ill. While not frail, she was old enough that I worried about the eye drops' effects on her. Of course, knowing Mrs. D'Angelo, she'd probably just order her body back to health, and it would comply out of sheer fear of the consequences of doing otherwise.

"No. That was actually the subject of the second cornering. The virtues of temperance."

I gasped. "You don't think she—"

"Poisoned everyone? Nah, she's a personality, but I don't think she's gone off the deep end. She actually seemed more offended that people were smoking."

"Smoking? At the party?" I may have been sick, but I wouldn't have missed the smell of cigarette smoke. It wasn't something you smelled much anymore, especially not indoors. I couldn't remember the last time I'd seen—or smelled—someone smoking indoors.

"Vaping, I think," Rhonda clarified. "I didn't see it, but she said something about 'those newfangled cigarettes.'" She slipped into a pitch-perfect imitation of Mrs. D'Angelo's upper-crust New England accent. "'They think they're getting away with something, but, mark my words, those things are just as much cancer sticks as the old kind.'" She dropped back into her own distinctly Massachusetts tones. "I mean, she's probably right. We've already talked to the boys a couple times about it. Not like they hear anything I say—in one ear and out the other. Dan has better luck, but that's because he mostly talks to them about sports."

We chatted for a few more minutes before hanging up. I wrote Mrs. D'Angelo's name down on my notepad in neat letters then stared at it for a while, tapping my pen on the paper. I had my list. Now I just needed to decide what to do with it. The right thing to do was to give it to Mike. He couldn't possibly be upset with me for making it when all I'd done was call my friends and ask them who they remembered seeing, could he?

I stared at the notepad a little longer and picked up my phone again. Slowly, I opened my list of contacts. My finger hovered over Mike's name. I knew I should tap it, but I did so only after a good bit of deliberation. There was no point in having made the list of names if I didn't turn it over to him, was there? It wasn't like there was anything I could do with it.

My call went straight to voicemail. I hung up without leaving a message, knowing that he'd see the missed call and call me back if he was so inclined. And if he didn't, that was his fault.

Still holding the phone, I looked at my list. Then back at the phone. I knew Mike didn't want me meddling in the case, but surely it couldn't hurt if I just made a couple of calls... Could it?

Chapter 21

MRS. D'ANGELO ANSWERED on the first ring. "D'Angelo residence," she said in her clipped tones.

"Hi, Mrs. D'Angelo, this is Fran Amaro—"

"Francesca! How lovely to hear from you! How are you, my dear? I heard about the incidents at your café! How awful! How terrifying that must be for you! I can't imagine what you must be going through! And that poor girl! Persephone, the paper said her name was. Such a lovely name but so tragic. You know your Greek mythology, I'm sure—"

She went on for several minutes about the ancient story of Persephone and how she was the cause of winter, and wasn't it just so poetic and her poor mother—Demeter, of course, not *our* Persephone's mother. She barely paused for breath and certainly not long enough for me to get a word in.

I started to worry that Mrs. D'Angelo would just hang up when she was done, as she did when she snagged you for one of her speeches out in public. She'd show up, grab onto your arm with her long nails, regale you with whatever she was thinking, and then disappear, leaving behind only the nail imprints in your arm and a cloud of heavy floral perfume.

"But I'm just on my way out to my Ladies' Auxiliary meeting. We're working on a fundraiser for the Cape Bay Historical Society—which I'm also a member of, of course. We're doing such good work. It was lovely talking to you, Francesca—"

I cut her off before she could hang up on me. "Actually, Mrs. D'Angelo, I wanted to ask you about my birthday party the other day."

The line went silent, and I thought that maybe I hadn't caught her in time—or that she'd hung up on me anyway. I had just pulled the phone away from my ear to see if the call was still connected when she finally spoke.

"Well, yes, dear, that's what we were just talking about. You received my donation, didn't you? I wrote quite a generous check—"

I interrupted her again, not wanting to give her the chance to really get going. "I don't know, actually. The police are holding it as evidence until the end of their investigation——"

She started huffing and puffing, but I didn't let her interrupt.

"I did know you attended, though, which I wanted to thank you for."

The huffing and puffing slowed down a little bit but didn't stop entirely.

"And I also wanted to make sure that you weren't affected by whatever made everyone else sick." On the spur of the moment, I decided to downplay my knowledge of the poison punch.

"Oh, no, dear, I abstain from all alcohol. And tobacco. I try to limit my vices as much as possible. An occasional dessert here or there——such as one of your lovely baked goods——but nothing too heavy or indulgent. It's not good for one's constitution to give in to temptation."

I was about to interrupt her again, but she kept plowing ahead.

"That was why I was so upset about those young people smoking! I told your girl about it, you know, the older brunette one, not young Samantha. Dean Howard and that Karli girl, Jack and Donna's daughter. I would have thought they raised her better than that, but who knows with children these days. Dean always was a handful. A bit of a disappointment to his father, but his mother was a pushover and never could discipline him. But regardless of upbringing, it's not appropriate for those people to be getting their nicotine fix in a public place, no matter how much they think it's okay because the cigarettes have computers in them now instead of lighting them with a match. Drugs are drugs, and I simply cannot tolerate their use in my presence. That was why they outlawed it. Well, not because of me personally, but because drugs shouldn't be used in public. It's a terrible example for the children. Why—"

I finally managed to get a word in. "Mrs. D'Angelo, didn't you say you were going somewhere? I wouldn't want you to be late because of me."

"Oh, goodness, yes! Thank you for reminding me! It was lovely speaking to you, Francesca. We really should catch up more often. Call me anytime. Bye-bye now!"

She hung up, and I tried to catch my breath from the whirlwind conversation. Talking to her was always dizzying, but it was somehow even more overwhelming over the phone. Maybe it was just the sheer effort of keeping up with the flood of words.

I took a stretch break and made myself a fresh latte with a swan as decoration this time. When I sat back down, I searched on my phone for the number for Todd's Gym and tapped it.

"Todd's Gym, this is Karli! How may I help you?" Karli sing-songed into the phone.

"Hi, Karli, this is Fran Amaro from Antonia's. How are you?"

"Oh." Her voice lost its professional cheeriness immediately. "Can I help you?"

"Um, I, um—" I hadn't really made a plan for the call, thinking I'd just engage in some friendly chitchat until I could direct the call the way I wanted, but Karli's coldness threw me off. "I just wanted—"

She sighed; her impatience was clear. I'd had enough of her. It wasn't worth trying. "Could I speak to Todd, please?"

"Does your boyfriend know how much you like to talk to Todd?"

Before I could formulate a response, I heard hold music. At least she hadn't hung up on me.

"This is Todd."

I stammered out a greeting and asked him how he was.

"Better than I was, that's for sure," he said, chuckling. "Whatever was in the punch was brutal! How about you? I heard about what happened to that girl who worked for you—what was her name? Emmy? Are you holding up okay?"

My stomach twisted in a knot. "I'm—I'm okay. It's a lot to deal with. It's—"

"Hang on a second, Fran."

There was a clatter that sounded like Todd putting the phone down on his desk.

"What's up, Kar?" I heard him say. There was a pause and then a sigh. "You know I don't like you doing that." Another pause. "I know, I know." Whoever he was talking to was far enough from the phone that I couldn't hear what they were saying, only Todd's responses. "No, I know. Look, I just wish you wouldn't, okay?" A sharp exhale. "Okay, fine, just try not to be gone too long, okay? Yeah, I'll cover the desk as soon as I'm done talking to Fran." After another heavy sigh, his voice came back louder on the line. "Sorry about that, Fran, where were we?"

"Everything okay?" I asked.

"Yeah. Yeah, just—" He groaned. "Between

you and me, Karli started vaping, and I hate it. It's a bad look for the gym to have her standing outside, sucking on a vape pen. Not to mention it's terrible for her. But her excuse is always that she's a grown woman and can do what she wants. How can I argue with that?"

I could think of a few things, but I wasn't sure any of them were in line with what Todd was thinking. Instead, I said what *I* was thinking. "Todd, are you and Karli seeing each other again?"

There was a long pause, during which I was sure I had offended him. Then, finally, "Don't tell her parents."

That sounded like something that would come out of the mouth of a sixteen-year-old rather than a thirty-six-year-old. Of course, sixteen was far closer to Karli's age than thirty-six.

"Why on earth would I tell them?" I asked.

"I dunno," Todd mumbled, again sounding more like a high-schooler than a successful business-man. "They'd just be furious if they found out."

"I won't breathe a word," I said.

I gave him a few more assurances and then managed to get off the phone. I wasn't sure what I had been trying to achieve with these phone calls— a spontaneous confession, maybe?—but so far I'd been chattered at by an elderly woman and then depressed by a middle-aged man. I still had a few names on my list, but I wasn't sure if it was worth hoping that those calls would go any better than the ones I'd already made.

Common sense (in other words, Matt and Mike) would probably tell me to give up, but common sense was something I was lacking in, so I used my phone to do an internet search for lawyers in Barnstable named Paul. Unfortunately, a name and a job weren't much to go on, especially when I wouldn't have recognized him in a picture. I gave up after about ten minutes.

I looked at the rest of my list and decided to call Melissa. She was fun and pleasant. A call to her would, if nothing else, boost my flagging spirits. Unfortunately, when she answered, the first words out of her mouth were that she was headed into her obstetrician's office. I let her go and continued down my list.

As I made my way through it, I refined my explanation for calling. I wanted to check in, see how they were feeling, thank them for coming to the party. Everyone was warm and pleasant, and to my chagrin, no one spontaneously confessed.

I was down to one name. Dean Howard. I'd

been putting off calling him because of how unpleasant our last interaction had been when I bumped into him at the café and almost spilled his coffee on him. I pulled up his number, took a deep breath, and tapped the green button.

"Howard!" he barked through the phone.

I put a smile on my face. "Hi, Dean, this is Fran Amaro, I just wanted to call and——"

"And what? Ask if I had gotten over the nasty case of food poisoning you gave me yet? Yes, I have. No thanks to you, of course."

I would have preferred to have all these conversations in person, but I was glad Dean couldn't see my face now. I had a feeling my smile had turned into a snarl. "I know, I'm so sorry about that——"

"And now the place is shut down again because someone died. Is that right?" Dean had always been a little rough around the edges, but now he was being surprisingly abrasive.

"Well, yes, but——"

"You know, maybe it's a good thing your little café is shut down. It seems like it's a dangerous place to be right now."

My mouth dropped open. I was stunned speechless.

"So, if you're not calling with an apology for all

my lost time, I'm gonna go. I have more important things to do than chitchat with you."

He hung up before I could splutter that I'd just apologized. And if that wasn't enough, I would be happy to apologize again.

I stared at the phone's screen until it went black and then put my head down on the table. I had spent the whole afternoon questioning people, and I had nothing to show for it. Well, nothing except a list of names that the police probably already had. I closed my eyes to rest, just for a minute. Matt would be home soon with dinner.

Chapter 22

I HEARD FOOTSTEPS AND SCREAMED. I grabbed hold of the first thing my hand landed on and jumped up, wielding it at the intruder. "Get out!" I screamed.

"Whoa, Franny!" Matt jumped back with his hands raised in the air, a white plastic bag dangling from one. "It's just me! With dinner! Put down the —phone? Why are you threatening me with a phone?"

I looked down at my hand and realized that the threatening object I'd grabbed from the table was a cell phone. Not the best weapon to use to fend off an intruder.

"Sorry," I said sheepishly.

His lips curled up in a smile that turned my

insides to goo and walked towards me. "No prob-lem, gorgeous." He pulled me close and kissed me on the forehead. "I brought burgers."

I had to get myself together before Matt killed us with an endless stream of greasy takeout. Even so, I was happy to tuck into the burgers sitting beside him at the kitchen table.

I was popping the last bite into my mouth when I noticed Matt looking down at the table with a curious expression. I followed his eyes and realized that I'd left my notepad out.

"What's this?" he asked, turning it so he could see it better.

"Just a list I made of people who were at our birthday party and at the café yesterday."

He looked at me.

I busied myself scraping the melted cheese off the burger's wrapper with my fingernail.

"Why were you making a list of those people? Did Mike ask you to?"

"Noooo," I said, drawing the word out. I scraped up some more of the cheese and sucked it off my finger.

"Franny."

I looked up and smiled hopefully. Maybe Matt would think the list was a good idea. Maybe he would be proud of me for showing initiative and being resourceful.

His frown said otherwise. "Franny, you know the police are working this case. You don't have to do it for them."

"I know. I just needed something to do. You told me not to just sit around!"

"I didn't mean to start investigating the case yourself." He sighed and leaned back in his chair. "I'm sorry. That probably sounded harsh. I think when I said to find something to do, I just pictured you baking or knitting or something."

"Knitting?" I'd never picked up a knitting needle in my life. I wasn't even sure if I'd know what one looked like if it was in front of me.

"I don't know. Something that normal people do. Something that's not murder-related." He reached out for the hand that hadn't been scraping cheese. "I just worry about you. You know that." He lifted my hand to his lips and kissed my fingertips. "I like you safe." A crooked smile crept across his face. "I guess that's one good thing about Mike putting you on lockdown. You can't go running around investigating clues and interviewing suspects." He chuckled.

I laughed, too, but it came out sounding a little

awkward and strangled. I hoped that he didn't notice.

"I guess making a list isn't too bad, after all. As long as you share the information with him. You are going to share the information with him, right?"

I nodded.

The pleasant, relaxed look on Matt's face slowly faded. "You were at home all day today, weren't you?"

I nodded again.

"And all you did was make this list?"

I looked down at the cheeseburger wrapper and studied it for any cheese I'd missed. "I called them," I muttered.

"I'm sorry? You *called* them?" I couldn't tell whether Matt's tone was one of disbelief or disapproval, but either way, it wasn't good. He rubbed his forehead with both hands.

"I wasn't weird about it," I said defensively. "I was just friendly! Asked how they were doing, apologized that people got sick, thanked them for coming. You know, nice, pleasant, neighborly stuff."

Matt looked doubtful.

"Really, it would have been rude not to call them. They came to our birthday party, and neither of us even got to speak to most of them. And then they got sick! I know if that happened to me, I'd appreciate it if my friend called to check on me."

"You can justify anything, can't you?" He undoubtedly had affection in his voice.

I shrugged. "I do a good job of it, don't I?"

He laughed and leaned across the table to kiss me. "Yeah, you do."

We cleaned up the trash from dinner and then retired to the living room to watch a couple of episodes of the latest show we'd been bingeing. Before long, we headed upstairs to bed. I'd say it was because we were both exhausted from a busy, overwhelming week, but that wouldn't be strictly accurate given how long it took for us to settle down to go to sleep.

Matt, of course, dropped off immediately, while I lay awake with my mind racing. Latte was lying between us, and I absently petted him while I thought about the conversations I'd had that day. Had anyone seemed suspect? Dean had been irrationally angry. Well, was it irrational? Maybe it was fair for him to be upset that he'd gotten so sick after coming to our party. It wasn't the way I would have reacted, but maybe it wasn't so off-the-wall.

Almost everyone had been pleasant and friendly. Karli had been a little snippy, but she seemed to think I was after Todd, although I couldn't think of why. I spoke to him when I saw him. That wasn't unusual. I spoke to most of the people I knew when I saw them. And I'd known Todd for longer than Karli had been alive! We went to high school together, for Pete's sake.

I put Karli out of my head. It had to be someone. Someone unexpected. Maybe the last person I expected.

I turned my head and looked at Matt in the darkness. Could *he* be trying to kill me? No, that was ridiculous. Why would Matt want to kill me? Unless he wanted to break up with me and couldn't figure out how. So he thought he'd just kill me instead? Get a grip, Fran.

I slipped out of bed. Latte raised his head and looked at me closely in case I was going downstairs to feed him.

"I'm just going to the bathroom, buddy."

He laid his head back down on the bed, but he followed me with his eyes. I padded across the bedroom and into the bathroom. While I was there, I got a drink of water and looked at myself in the mirror, trying to clear my head. There was no way Matt was trying to kill me, especially not in such convoluted ways. Matt was a professional engineer.

He was smart enough to actually kill me if he wanted to. At that bizarre thought, I turned off the bathroom light and headed back to bed.

I crawled in and forced myself to close my eyes. It didn't work. They popped right back open. I stared at the ceiling for a while. It still had the remnants of the glow-in-the-dark stars my mom and I had stuck to it when I was a kid. My mom had wanted to put them in the shapes of constellations and started off that way, but I didn't have the patience to wait for her to carefully align them and ended up sticking them wherever I could reach, which ended up being mostly in a six-inch blob. My mom, my wonderful mom, had looked momentarily dismayed, but then she smiled and gave me a hug, telling me my work was beautiful. I missed her so much.

I rolled over and shut my eyes again. This time, instead of thinking about who might be trying to kill me, I thought about my mom. We'd had our ups and downs like all mothers and daughters, but what I wouldn't give for one more day with her. We'd had so many good times in this house and at the café while I was growing up. Her bedroom had been right across the hall, my grandparents' at the bottom of the stairs. It was a good way to grow up. The best way, as far as I was concerned.

My eyes popped open. Was that a squeak? It sounded like the creak of the stairs. I rolled over and put my hand on Latte. Had he made a sound? He did that sometimes, when he was dreaming. Quiet little woofs or squeaks. His legs would twitch just a little as he dreamt of running on the beach or chasing squirrels. He wasn't moving now, but maybe my turning over had jostled him out of his dream.

I closed my eyes again. It was just Latte. He made little noises all the time. My body had just relaxed when I startled awake again.

This time there was no mistaking it.

Someone was coming up the stairs.

Chapter 23

"MATT," I hissed. "Matt, wake up." I swatted at him to try to awaken him. He grunted and rolled over.

I poked Latte, hoping he would wake up and notice the intruder. He wiggled closer to Matt and ignored me.

The stairs creaked again. I took a deep, shaky breath and tried to think of what to do. I could get up and confront them, but they could be armed. Or I could stay put and wait for them to come in the bedroom. Neither option seemed good.

I listened for another creak. This house was an older one, so most of the stairs had some sort of squeak or groan, but I knew from youthful experience that the second from the top was the worst. On the few occasions that teenage me had snuck into the house late at night, I'd always skipped that one. In fact, I'd had a whole system for creeping up the stairs as noiselessly as possible. It was usually wasted on me watching TV later than I was supposed to or, worse, staying up late studying, but I'd had a system. A system that whoever was walking up the stairs now had no idea about, thank goodness.

I nudged Latte again, but this time I whispered the magic word. "Treat!" Latte immediately lifted his head and looked at me. "Treat!" I whispered again, this time pointing at the door.

Latte jumped up and leapt off the bed, heading for the door at a full gallop. As soon as he got through the door, he started barking frantically at whoever was on the steps. I suddenly worried that I'd sent him into danger.

Fortunately, almost immediately, I heard feet pounding down the creaky stairs, accompanied by Latte's paws clattering down behind them. The front door banged against the wall behind it, and Latte's barks grew more distant.

I crept out of bed and poked my head out the door to look down the stairs. The stairs were empty, and the door was wide open. Latte was framed in it, silhouetted by the dim moonlight. He was still barking into the night.

I went back across the room and grabbed my phone from where it was charging on the nightstand. With shaking hands, I dialed 911.

Matt sat up just as the 911 operator answered. "What's going on?"

My response was to the operator. "Hi, I'd like to report a break-in."

THIRTY MINUTES LATER, the street was filled with flashing red and blue lights. My house was filled with police officers.

Matt was on the couch, wearing a T-shirt and sweatpants he'd hastily thrown on when he finally woke up enough to process what was going on. Latte was curled up beside him, back asleep after his stint as a guard dog. He'd used up a lot of energy barking furiously at every single police officer who had come through the door. Except for Mike. Latte liked Mike.

I was manning the espresso machine in the kitchen, using my plentiful mug collection to make cups of coffee for all the officers who'd been roused out of sleep to come search my house for signs of the intruder.

Mike paced around, barking orders at the officers, not all of whom were even Cape Bay police. I'd spotted at least one state police uniform and a couple of uniforms from the sheriff's office. It seemed like a little bit of overkill, even to me, but at least Mike had stopped short of calling in the National Guard.

"Fran, we're ready for you!" Mike shouted from the living room.

"Just a second! I have two more drinks to make."

"Fran!" He had a warning tone in his voice, but I didn't care.

"Mike!" I replied in the same tone.

I didn't know what had gotten into me. While the earlier threats had scared me into stillness, leaving me curled up on the couch in terror for parts of two days, someone actually breaking in had lit a fire under me, and I was dealing with it in the best way I knew how—by making coffee. And I wasn't going to stop until every last officer had gotten a cup.

I finished the cup I was making and decorated it with a rosetta. I would have liked to do something more elaborate, but I felt like it wasn't the time. I put the mug on the table and called over to the officer brushing the back door for fingerprints to let him know his coffee was ready. He waved a hand in thanks and went back to his careful work.

"One more!" I called to Mike before he could call me again.

I smiled at the officer who was waiting. "Latte okay?"

"I drink gas station coffee ninety percent of the time," she said with a smile. "I can stomach whatever you give me."

"Well, hopefully, this is a little better than gas station quality." I pulled her shot of espresso and then carefully poured the milk in. As I handed her cup over, I leaned in. "By the way, your bun is falling out."

Her hand flew to where a chunk of her hair had slipped out of its elastic and was hanging down past her uniform collar. "Oh, gosh, thank you!"

"Bathroom's over there." I pointed through the kitchen to the powder room. She put her coffee down on the counter and took off that way.

I wiped my hands on a towel and went out into the living room, plopping myself down on the couch next to Matt. "Okay, I'm ready," I said, smiling at Mike. He'd sat down in his usual chair with his notebook resting on the makeshift table created by his ankle crossed over his opposite knee.

He and Matt exchanged a look.

"Okay, Fran, can you tell me what happened?" he asked. His eyes were puffy with sleep. I had a feeling that he could fall back asleep in a heartbeat, despite the Americano I'd greeted him at the door with.

I quickly told him about the noise on the stairs, me trying to wake Matt and Latte up, and how I'd finally gotten Latte to chase the intruder out of the house.

"Matt, does that line up with what you observed?"

"Uhh—" Matt looked around uncomfortably. "I slept through the whole thing."

Mike's smirk told me he already knew that and was enjoying the opportunity to mess with Matt. Professional officer of the law he might have been, but he still wasn't going to miss the opportunity to give his buddy grief.

"I want you to think back. Did you hear anything before the creak on the stairs? The door maybe? Any movement downstairs?"

I thought back. "No. I was trying to go to sleep, so I may have already drifted off."

Mike nodded and jotted down some notes. "And you, Matt?"

"Not a thing. I was asleep."

"Did either of you lock the door before you went upstairs?"

"Of course!" I said. Then I stopped. It had been locked all day—I knew because I'd checked both the front and back doors several times. But had I checked it before bed? I wasn't sure. "Actually, I don't think I did."

"Matt?"

"Well, I was awake for that!" he said proudly. "But I have no idea. I probably locked it, but I'm not really sure."

Cape Bay was a small enough town that a lot of people still had the habit of leaving their doors unlocked and their car keys in the ignition. My years living in New York City had thoroughly broken me of that habit, but I still caught Matt forgetting from time to time.

"Keep a key under the doormat?"

"No," I said firmly.

Mike looked mildly surprised. Like I said, most

Cape Bayers didn't place a high priority on securing their property.

"I keep an extra at the café."

"But how will you get into the café if your keys are locked inside the house?" Matt asked.

"Sammy." We really needed to have another talk about how to properly secure our homes.

Mike turned around in his chair. "Hey, Molloy!"

A crime scene tech crouching at the foot of the stairs looked up with a pair of tweezers in his hand. I caught a glint of what looked like dog hair in it.

"Make sure your people check all the points of entry for signs of force. And check the locks for fingerprints."

"Of course, Detective." Molloy dropped the hair into a bag and plucked another one from the carpet. I really needed to vacuum more.

"I'll send someone to check the café, just in case. You have an alarm, right?"

I confirmed that I did.

He spoke into his police radio. "Hey, Leary, if you're not busy, could you roll by Antonia's and check the front and back doors?"

The voice of Sammy's boyfriend crackled through. "Sure thing, Detective."

Mike looked back at me. "I doubt they gained

access using the key at the café. That would take a lot of planning, which doesn't seem like this guy's strong suit. And the alarm would have gone off. But we'll make sure."

The front door swung open as another cop made his way in. Latte, who hadn't moved since I'd come out of the kitchen, jumped up and started barking ferociously. The cop put his hands up and started backing out the way he came.

Mike chuckled. "Well, if I had any doubts that this guy could scare off a burglar, they're gone now."

"Sit, Latte!" I commanded.

He climbed across Matt and stood on my lap.

"Little protector you got there." Mike chuckled.

"At least somebody has my back," I said, looking pointedly at Matt. His eyes got big, and I patted his leg. "Just teasing."

"You guys aren't going to let this go, are you?" Matt asked.

"Nope," Mike and I said together.

"Detective?" The cop who Latte had tried to scare off was still standing at the doorway.

"Come on in," Mike said. "The dog's mostly harmless."

As soon as the cop put one foot across the threshold, Latte's barking started up again.

"Maybe you'd better come to me, sir?"

Mike chuckled and stood up. He stepped towards me. I expected Latte's barking to erupt again, but I guess he really did like Mike because he just stood there. Mike reached out and scratched Latte's head. "Good boy." Latte licked his hand. "I don't know what that dog has against you, Simons." Mike laughed as he walked towards the door. Over his shoulder, he told me and Matt that he'd be back.

"I'm sorry I didn't wake up," Matt said, for possibly the hundredth time since he'd awoken to me on the phone with the police.

"It's okay." I patted him on the leg again. "You're here now. That's what matters."

"What matters is that I almost let us get murdered because I didn't wake up when you needed me."

"It's fine, Matty. *We're* fine."

He pulled his phone out of his pocket and started tapping.

"What are you doing?"

"I'm ordering you an alarm system."

"I don't need an alarm system."

"Apparently, you do," he retorted.

I sighed and let him keep tapping. If it would make him feel better to get me an alarm system, I'd let him.

Mike came back after a few minutes and sat back down in his chair. He looked from Matt to me. "So."

"So?" It was only one syllable, but I didn't like the sound of it.

"I'm not going to sugarcoat this. This break-in concerns me. Assuming it's the same perpetrator, I don't like this kind of escalation in behavior. Until now, the attacks have been passive—traps set for you to fall into. Coming into your home—while you're sleeping, no less—is much more aggressive behavior. What also concerns me is the time frame we're seeing. In, let's say, a stalking case, you'd expect to see escalation like this over the course of months or even years. This has been less than a week. It worries the hell out of me. So."

That same deep-seated fear I'd felt clench at my stomach after Ephy's death grabbed onto me again. "So?" I prompted, even though I wasn't sure I wanted to hear what was coming next.

"Until now, I was hopeful that the café was more of a target than you specifically."

My mind shot to Dean's bitterness and the way

he'd suggested it was good that the café was shut down.

"But the perpetrator actually coming into your home changes the equation. Without a doubt, you are the target." He stopped and took a deep breath, making eye contact with me and then Matt in turn. I actually thought he even made eye contact with Latte, but that must have been my imagination.

"Effective immediately, I'm stationing officers at your front and back doors until we have this case solved."

"What?"

He held up a hand to stop me. "I told you to stay home before, but I want to reiterate now that you are not to leave this house. I don't want you to so much as step foot outside the door."

"What about Latte?"

"My officers will supervise him going outside."

"That's ridiculous! You're putting police officers in charge of my dog's potty breaks?" This time, my fear wasn't making me cower on the couch. It was making me mad.

"I'm putting police officers in charge of your safety, and right now that means keeping you inside no matter what," Mike said sternly.

"I need groceries. I have nothing in the house."

"Matt can buy you groceries."

I fumed silently while I tried to think of another good excuse for me to go out. "What about the café?"

"It's staying closed for now."

"I have a lot of food that will go bad if we don't open."

"Leary can take Sammy over to clear out anything perishable. She can either take it home for herself or bring it to you."

"What about—"

Mike put his hand up. "That's enough. There are no exceptions."

"You can't do this. You can't unilaterally put me on house arrest!" I knew arguing wasn't going to do any good, but I couldn't stop myself.

"No, I can't, but I'm asking you to do what I say for your own protection."

I inhaled to argue some more, but Matt put his hand on my leg to stop me. "Franny. He's right. You know he's right. It's not safe. You're staying at home."

I started to snap at him that he couldn't tell me what to do, but the tender look in his eyes sapped some of my frustration. I sighed. "Okay, fine. I'll stay at home."

"Thank you," Mike said. "And I wanted to tell you, we finally tracked down Ephy's relative. She's only got an aunt in Maine, and they're not close. Ephy's grandmother had been the one to raise her, and she'd passed away last year."

"Poor thing," I said, sniffling.

Mike nodded grimly. "So it's up to the aunt whether she'll hold a funeral, but likely not. She didn't sound like she knew Ephy well."

I put my hands over my face. That poor young woman. I didn't know what happened to her parents, and with her grandma gone, she had been all alone. Now her own life was gone. And there was nothing I could do about it.

"Do you have any other questions before I go and let you get back to sleep?"

I glanced around, surprised to see that most of the officers who'd been swarming my house had disappeared.

"Actually, Mike, there is. While she was at home today—"

I snapped my head toward Matt as I realized what he was about to say. Mercifully, he stopped talking. Unfortunately, Mike had caught our little exchange.

"What?"

"It's nothing. It's not important," I said.

Mike obviously didn't believe me. He looked at Matt.

I sighed. I knew he'd never let it go. "Go ahead."

"Franny made a list of everyone who was at the party and was also at the café yesterday."

"Okay. We've done the same thing, but if you want to share your list—"

Matt cut Mike off. "And then she called them all."

Mike closed his eyes. "You. Called. All the people who had the opportunity to commit both attacks?" he said slowly.

"Yes?" I braced for his reaction.

Luckily for me, it was mild. He just leaned back in the armchair, covered his eyes, and groaned.

Chapter 24

THE NEXT DAY, I found myself yet again alone in my house. Matt had argued and debated, but he finally conceded that he did need to go in to work. And so there I was, just Latte and me. And a police officer at the front and back doors. And one down the street in an unmarked car. And possibly another one somewhere that I didn't know about. It seemed like overkill to me, but Mike was afraid the attacks would continue to escalate, and he didn't want to take any chances.

My anger from the previous night had dissipated, but it had been replaced by a nervous energy that made it impossible for me to sit still. All the coffee I'd had probably didn't help. I'd started with a cup for myself and one for each of the officers outside. By the time I'd delivered their cups and engaged in some polite chitchat, I was ready for my next cup, which I drank while wandering around the house, trying to figure out what I should spend my time doing. I ended up deciding to make myself another cup of coffee.

Then I deep cleaned the espresso machine.

Then I took everything off the counters, gave the counters a good cleaning, wiped down everything that had been on them, and put everything back neatly.

Then I cleaned the cabinet doors.

Then I wiped down the kitchen table and chairs.

It was barely lunchtime.

I usually ate at the café, so I didn't have much in the way of ingredients. Still, I managed to throw together a quick spaghetti carbonara with some good Italian pasta, pancetta, Pecorino Romano cheese, eggs, and black pepper—simple things I pretty much always had in the house. I delivered some to the officers at the doors then sat down and ate the rest.

I washed the dishes and checked the time. It had barely taken an hour.

I made myself another latte.

Standing in the middle of the kitchen, fueled by nerves and caffeine, I looked around for what to tackle next. I decided on the cabinets. There were a few pots and pans I used on a regular basis, but I hadn't really emptied everything out to assess what was inside since I inherited the house after my mother's death.

And so that was how Matt ended up finding me sitting in the middle of the kitchen floor, surrounded by sixty or so years of kitchen utensils, when he came home with takeout tacos for dinner.

"So, how was your day?" he asked casually, looking around at the disaster that was my kitchen.

"I've been working on reorganizing the kitchen," I replied.

"I see that," he said slowly. He held up the bag in his hand. "I have tacos."

I looked around, briefly considering asking him to just hand me the tacos so I could eat them where I was. My grandparents and my mom had accumulated quite a lot of cooking vessels in their time in the house, not to mention the things I'd brought back with me from New York. Finally, I just started pushing things aside—carefully, so as not to disturb the organization system I'd started. Matt worked from the other side and then reached out his hand to help pull me up.

I glanced in the direction of the espresso machine, thinking another latte would be tasty with dinner, but the path to it was covered by colanders of various shapes and sizes. I'd have to make do with—well, water from the upstairs bathroom in my dirty coffee cup, since I couldn't make it to the sink either.

We ate our tacos picnic-style on the living room floor, watching my baking show that Matt had somehow become invested in. His baking knowledge and interest was usually limited to "what did you make?" and "what's in it?" and "can I have some?" but he suddenly had opinions on the proper way to fold a mousse and whether Viennese whirls needed to be refrigerated between piping and baking. I'd created a monster. I loved it.

But when I was in bed that night, the sinking fear that someone was trying to kill me settled back in. Who could want me dead? Mike—and Matt for that matter—seemed to think I'd triggered someone to break in when I made my calls the day before. Someone thought I was more suspicious of them than I was. I thought about who I'd talked to—

Todd, Dean, Melissa for barely a second, Karli for hardly longer than that.

The thought dawned on me that they'd all been closely involved in a murder since I'd come back to town the year before. Melissa's ex-boyfriend, who was also the father of her oldest child, had been murdered in the parking lot of Todd's Gym. That hadn't really involved Karli, but she did work at the front desk. It had been a stressful time for everyone at the gym. And then one of Dean's employees had died during a break-in at his jewelry store. Could any of them be holding a grudge against me for my role in investigating those crimes? It was possible— but who? And why?

I drifted off to sleep before I could think about it anymore.

THE NEXT DAY was more of the same. I immediately cleared a path to the espresso machine and was on my third cup of coffee before I made it back to my kitchen organization. Sleep and a fresh infusion of caffeine had it going more quickly than it had the previous afternoon. I got everything organized and put away by lunch, except for a cast-iron skillet I'd found that I set aside for Sammy. She'd mentioned wanting one, and I had never used the one I didn't even know I had, so I wanted to give it to her.

Mike called around lunchtime with an update on the case, or at least what he called an update anyway. All he really said was that they were looking into leads and would keep me posted. And I was still to stay at home, despite my best efforts at convincing him to let me out.

I started getting antsy again around midafternoon and convinced the back door officer—a different one from yesterday—to let me play fetch with Latte. I was allowed provided I kept both feet indoors at all times. Apparently, Mike had been serious about not even setting a foot outside.

By midafternoon the next day, I had cleaned out the refrigerator and pantry and made a detailed shopping list for Matt. Immediately after dinner—pizza again—I sent him to the grocery store to stock up. I made him video-chat me anytime he wasn't sure exactly which product to get so that I could approve a replacement. The last time I'd asked him to pick up flour at the grocery store, he came back with the self-rising kind, and I wasn't willing to risk that again.

The day after that I spent baking. I prepped

enough puff pastry for about a year, wrapped almost all of it up tightly and froze it. That was one great thing about puff pastry—it froze incredibly well. I took the portion I'd set aside and used it to make chocolate rolls, which I shared with the officers staking out my house. I put a few prepared rolls in the fridge to bake for dessert, since I knew how much they loved them. I baked some bread, started a batch of brioche, and made chicken parmesan for dinner. By the time Matt got home, dinner was on the table, the house was immaculate, and I was bored out of my mind.

"I called Mike today," I said as we sat down to dinner. I had just popped the chocolate rolls in the oven and figured they'd be out and cool just in time for dessert.

"Oh yeah?" Matt had already cut a tender piece of chicken off with his fork and stuffed it in his mouth. "Chicken's delicious."

"Thank you." I took a bite myself. I had to admit—I'd done a good job.

"So what did you and Mike talk about?" he asked after enough time that I thought he'd forgotten.

"I just asked him to come by tonight."

Matt put his fork down. "Why?"

"I just want to see how the investigation's going." I twirled some spaghetti onto my fork and popped it into my mouth.

He looked at me with suspicion. "You couldn't ask that over the phone?"

I smiled. "I've been stuck in this house for days on Mike's orders. I feel like coming by to update me in person is the least he can do."

"Fair enough," he said without looking like he believed me at all.

We finished our dinner just as Mike knocked on the door. As always, his knock was more of a bang that could scare the life out of you if you weren't expecting it. I actually was expecting it and still jumped out of my chair.

The oven timer went off just as Matt opened the door for Mike.

"What smells like chocolate?" Mike asked.

"Franny made dessert," Matt said.

"Save me any dinner?"

I suddenly wondered if I should have made him a portion as well. The question must have shown on my face because Mike immediately smiled.

"Just kidding, Franny. Sandra'll have dinner for

me at home, which is where I'm finally going right after this."

"The chocolate rolls just need to cool for a few minutes," I said, coming into the living room and sitting down on the couch. Matt and Mike had already taken their seats. Latte was leaning on Mike's leg, getting his hair all over Mike's dress pants. Mike seemed okay with it, though—he was leaned over, giving Latte double-handed scratches.

"So, what's up, Franny?" he asked as Latte lifted his hand.

"I was just hoping for an update on the case," I replied cheerfully.

Matt and Mike both looked at me with skepticism, but Mike gamely answered. "Not much to report, unfortunately. We've been tracking down leads, but there's not much evidence. The best we got was a single hair from your steps, but without a DNA sample to compare it to, it doesn't give us much. If we identify a suspect, we can use it to confirm that they were here, but without one, we're out of luck."

"*If* you identify a suspect?" Matt asked.

Mike sighed. "Unfortunately, that's where we are."

"So can I go back to work?" I asked.

Like they shared one brain, they simultaneously burst out with "No!"

"So, what's your plan, then? You're just going to keep me here until someone spontaneously confesses?"

"No, of course not," Mike said. Matt, on the other hand, looked like he would consider it.

"Then what?"

"Fran, I'm just not comfortable relaxing the police protection just yet."

I stood up. "Fine, then I'm just going to solve the case from here."

"We will solve it. You just need to give us time," Mike said.

"You can't do that, Franny," Matt said at the same time.

I stomped into the kitchen and threw some of the chocolate rolls in a storage container. I took them back into the living room and shoved them at Mike. "Here. Take these and go."

He looked at me in stunned surprise.

"Go!"

"Franny—" Matt stood up and put his hand on my arm, but I didn't take my eyes off Mike.

"If you don't have any other news about the case, you can go ahead and go. There's no reason to keep you when you obviously have work you could be doing."

Latte looked wounded as Mike stopped petting him and stood up. He took the storage container from me.

"Franny—" Matt started again.

"No, Matt, it's fine. She has every right to be upset." He moved toward the door. "Thanks for the, uh—" He peered into the container.

"Chocolate rolls," I said. "Puff pastry chocolate rolls."

"The chocolate rolls. Thank you." He nodded to Matt and went out the door.

That night, Matt and I had the biggest fight we'd ever had and, frankly, that I hoped we'd ever have. I yelled that he wasn't in charge of me, and he yelled that he was just worried about my safety. I countered that I was going stir-crazy. He said that it was just for a little while. I pointed out that he had gotten to leave the house every day and interact with other human beings while I'd been stuck inside with a (truly excellent) dog and only occasionally got to talk to the police officers stationed outside. He said the police were taking care of it. I shouted that they clearly were not. He yelled that they were working on it. I said that it wasn't fast enough. He bellowed that I needed to leave it alone. I screamed that he couldn't tell me what to do, and if that was what he was going to do, he could get out of my house. He left and went home. I cried myself to sleep.

Chapter 25

I WOKE up to my phone ringing. I picked it up and looked at the screen, hoping it was Matt calling to apologize, but the display had Mike's name on it. I silenced the ringer, put the phone down, and rolled over to go back to sleep.

A minute later, I heard the ding of the voicemail notification. And then the chime of a text message. I rolled over to put the phone on silent before he could annoy me any further, but the text message caught my eye. *Call me.* It wasn't much, but it was something.

Reluctantly, I called Mike back.

"Hey, Fran, how you doin' this morning?" he said, greeting me with more enthusiasm than I could handle.

I felt awful. I felt sad and emotionally exhausted. I felt unmoored, unbalanced. I felt like I had a hangover without having drunk a single glass the night before. But I didn't think Mike wanted all that dumped on him first thing in the morning. "I'm okay. How are you?"

"I think you're going to be a lot better than okay in a minute."

"Did you find out who's trying to kill me?"

There was a pause, and I realized I had probably overshot my optimism.

"Okay, not *that* much better. But I think you are going to be happy."

Couldn't he just get to the point already?

"I'm letting you reopen the café."

I sat up in bed, jolting Latte out of his slumber. He immediately looked toward the door with a growl.

"Please say you're not just messing with me. I can't handle it if you're just messing with me."

"I'm not messing with you," he said with a chuckle. "Now, I'm not completely letting you loose, but you can reopen."

"That's great! Today? It's already a little late, but—"

"Not today. I still need to get some security worked out, and we need to discuss some things."

"So, tomorrow?" I asked hopefully.

"Tomorrow should be fine."

"Great!" My mind started racing with all the things I needed to do to get ready to reopen. "I'll need to go to the store for some supplies and—"

"Not so fast," Mike interrupted. "We still need to prioritize your safety and security. You'll need to get someone else to pick up whatever supplies you need."

Slightly defeated, I asked what the other rules were. He gave me a rundown. No going anywhere alone. No going anywhere without notifying him or another officer. No eating or drinking anything I didn't personally prepare using freshly opened ingredients. Above all, no investigating. If I so much as got a flicker of an inclination to stick my nose anywhere that it didn't belong, I was to shove that inclination out of my head faster than I could down a shot of espresso. Mike's words, not mine, of course. I didn't shoot espresso—I sipped it so I could appreciate the nuances of its flavor. It wasn't quite the way I would have liked things to go, but it was better than staying locked in the house all the time. I agreed to all his conditions.

"There's one more thing," he said, just as I thought we were about to hang up. "Whoever's behind these attacks has been lying low for the past few days. That could mean that they've given up, and you won't have any more problems with them. Or it could mean that the police presence has been enough to deter them. If we scale back, they could come after you again. And we already know how dangerous they can be. Are you sure you want to do this?"

I took a deep breath. His warning was enough to give me pause but not enough to scare me off. I was ready to have my life back. "I'm sure."

"I had a feeling that would be your answer." I could hear the smile in his voice. "You work on getting things ready to reopen tomorrow. Only things you can do from home. Anything else, you'll have to get Sammy or Rhonda to handle. I'll come by later tonight to make sure we're clear on how everything's going to work, okay?"

"Sounds good. Oh, and Mike?" I stopped him before he could hang up. "I'm sorry for kicking you out like that last night. I was frustrated and just... not at my best. I'm sorry."

"No hard feelings. And if there were, those chocolate roll things would have made up for it.

Sandra and I finished them off last night. One of the best things you've ever made."

I thanked him, and we hung up. My first instinct was to call Matt to tell him the good news. I even got as far as pulling his number up on my phone, but I stopped before I hit the call button. I still had too many feelings about our fight the night before.

I called Sammy instead. Together, we worked out a plan for what we needed to do to get the café ready to reopen. Sammy was responsible for picking up any of the supplies we needed to replace, and I was responsible for... well, not much, since I was still technically not supposed to leave the house. But I could still coordinate coverage and plan the bakes and drink specials for the day. I was tempted to put everything on special to celebrate our reopening but restrained myself to a spring-themed latte and a buy-one-get-one-free donut deal. I still wasn't comfortable having Becky and Amanda come in, so I arranged for Sammy to open and Rhonda to close. I planned to be there all day.

Most of the day was spent brainstorming and making calls, either to Sammy and Rhonda to coordinate details, or to our suppliers to see if they could rearrange deliveries so we could have as much of our normal stock as possible. I barely had time to think about the fight Matt and I had gotten in. Well, I could barely think about it if you defined "barely" as hardly being able to keep it off my mind and needing to continue finding distracting tasks.

There was one thing I actually didn't think about, not until long after Mike had explained that I'd still have to have police protection, just inside my house instead of stationed outside it, as well as another officer lurking behind the scenes at the café. That was that someone was trying to kill me.

That thought held off until I was lying in bed, Latte at my side, trying not to think about Matt. Then, suddenly, it was all I could think about. Someone was trying to kill me. Someone wanted me dead.

I realized that I had mentally narrowed the suspects down to Dean and Todd. Dean because he seemed to have such a grudge against me and Todd because, well, I couldn't think of many reasons why Todd would be out to get me. I'd helped solve the murder outside his gym, which should have been a good thing. I'd figured out that he and Karli were dating, which eventually led to her parents making them break up, but Todd and Karli were back together now, so that shouldn't matter.

Thinking about Todd and Karli's relationship got me thinking about Matt again. I hadn't talked to him all day. It was the longest we'd gone without talking since we'd been together. I wished I was brave enough to call him and apologize. He was probably still furious with me. He'd be even more furious if he knew I was going back to work tomorrow. But I missed him so much.

I WAS up before the sun the next morning without an alarm, excited and raring to go. I grabbed the cast-iron skillet I'd set aside for Sammy and tucked it into my tote bag. Sammy's boyfriend, Officer Ryan Leary, was waiting outside my front door for me. He introduced me to the officer who would be guarding my house while I was gone. I gave her a brief explanation of how to use the espresso machine and invited her to make herself at home. Ryan escorted me to the café, where Sammy was already waiting. She gave me a big hug and Ryan a kiss. After I gave her the skillet, Ryan settled into the back room, where he'd be stationed for the day, and Sammy and I got to work.

We made donuts and baked cookies. I mixed up

some brownies and popped them in the oven. Sammy threw together a quick soda bread and got it baking. We sliced tomatoes and chopped lettuce and got a decent amount of preparation done before the first early-morning patrons started trickling into the café.

Everyone was ecstatic that we were open again. Customer after customer gave us hugs. They expressed their sympathies at Ephy's death and their gratitude that we were alive. I tried not to feel too guilty.

Mike came by more often than was strictly necessary. I wasn't sure that even he could drink as much coffee as he was downing. He'd come in, get a cup, then wander back out to make a loop of Main Street before wandering in again. I almost pointed out that he was being far from sneaky, but I didn't want to do anything that would endanger my ability to stay open, so I kept my mouth shut and kept filling his cup.

Mid-morning, Dean came in, scowling, and got a donut and a cappuccino to go. I watched from the end of the counter as Sammy told him that the donuts were buy-one-get-one. "One is plenty," he snapped. He took his bag and glared at me on the way out. I didn't know why he came in if he was so grumpy about it.

It was shortly after lunchtime when Todd came in. I'd gotten so used to seeing him with Karli glued to his hip that I was surprised to see him by himself. He gave me a big hug when he saw me. "Fran! I'm so glad you're open again. I've been so worried about you."

"You have?" I asked, genuinely not expecting to hear that. "Why?"

"You know." He shrugged. "Just everything that's been going on."

He looked down at me with his sparkly blue eyes, his hands still resting on my shoulders. I searched his face for any sign of malice but came up empty. I couldn't imagine that Todd had anything against me.

"Todd? What are you doing here?"

Todd dropped his hands from my shoulders as he turned and saw his girlfriend. "Karli! Hey. I thought I'd stop in to see Fran now that Antonia's is open again."

She looked from Todd to me in disgust. I wanted to tell her that I was not interested in her boyfriend, not by a long shot. I had my own boyfriend. He and I might have been going through a rough patch, but I wasn't looking to trade him in. Instead, I just gave her a warm smile. "Hi, Karli!"

She ignored me and looked at Todd. "I was going to surprise you with a coffee." She pouted.

"How about I buy you one instead?" He wrapped his arm around her bare shoulders. Winter was definitely over, but I didn't know how she wasn't cold in her layered tank tops (blue and green today).

"Okay." She pursed her lips and tipped her head up. Todd glanced at me sheepishly before giving her a quick kiss. I was surprised that they were being so openly affectionate when they were still trying to hide their relationship from Karli's parents. She turned to me triumphantly. "I want a large iced latte with extra vanilla syrup."

I nodded with my best attempt at a bland, neutral smile. I didn't want to do anything that she might construe as passing judgement on her drink choice.

I made her drink and gave Todd the black coffee he ordered. They left the café with their arms around each other, and I turned to greet the next customer.

Chapter 26

I HAD PLANNED to stay at the café from open to close, but around late afternoon, I started to flag. Thirteen hours was a long time to be cheerfully greeting people who might want me dead. Sammy was gone, but Rhonda had come in, and business was slow.

"Why don't you just go home?" Rhonda asked. "I can handle the rest of the day."

"I'm fine. I was at home for days," I replied.

The truth was that as long as I was busy at the café, I wasn't thinking about how Matt and I hadn't spoken in almost forty-eight hours. Every time I thought about it, I felt nauseous and doubled down on my work.

"Fran. Seriously. Go home. You don't need to be here. I've got this."

I looked around at the few occupied tables and sighed. Even my level of stubbornness had its limits. "Okay, fine." I pulled my apron over my head and gave her a hug. "Call me if it gets busy."

"Will do, chief." She gave me a mock salute.

I went in the back and hung up my apron. Ryan had been relieved around midday, and I told his replacement I was ready to go home for the night.

"Sure thing," he said. "I'll let Detective Stanton know." He started tapping on his phone.

I grabbed my purse, and I noticed that Sammy had forgotten her skillet. I'd have to remind her tomorrow and make sure she knew that it was a gift. I didn't need it back.

My cell phone dinged as I put my bag on my shoulder. I pulled it out, expecting some kind of warning from Mike to be careful, but I saw Matt's name on the screen. And underneath, *I love you. I'm sorry.*

I replied immediately. *I'm sorry too. I love you.*

His reply came back before I could even put my phone away. *Romantic dinner for two tonight at Fiesta?*

My mouth dropped open.

His next message popped up. *Mike told me he set you free ;)*

My reply was one word. *YES*

I felt like I was floating on air as the officer escorted me home. I'd had a good day back at the café, and Matt and I had kissed and made up. Well, we'd made up. The kissing would come later.

Latte greeted me at the door like I'd been gone for ten days instead of ten hours.

The officer inside grinned at me. "He's the best stakeout partner I've ever had!"

"He's a good boy! Yes he is! Yes he is!" My voice descended into doggie-talk as I got down on my knees to give him good scratches. "Can I take him for a walk?" I asked the officer.

"Let me arrange it," she said.

"Arrange what?" I asked.

"Someone to tail you. Detective's orders. You're not allowed out alone."

I sighed and played with Latte for a few minutes while I waited for the officer to tell me I could go.

Finally, she nodded. "Okay, you can go. Go right at the end of your front walk. There's an officer waiting at the end of the block to the left. He'll be following you the whole time but at a distance. His job is to blend in, so don't worry if you look back and don't see him. If you do start to get worried, call him. I'll give you his number."

I programmed the officer's phone number into my cell and made sure it was ready to call if I needed to. "Anything else?" I asked her.

"Enjoy your walk!"

I hooked Latte's leash onto his collar and headed out. At the end of my front walk, I glanced to the left. At the end of a block, a man in jeans and a T-shirt was staring down at his phone. I glanced at my front window. I couldn't see her, but I knew the officer inside was watching. I took a deep breath, turned to the right, and started walking.

The day was glorious. The sun was shining, the birds were singing in the trees, and a light breeze brought the scent of the ocean to my nose. It was the first time I'd been alone and outside of my house in days.

At the corner, I turned right to go toward Main Street and the beach. I'd forgotten to bring a ball to use for fetch on the beach, but we could walk along the boardwalk. It usually had enough people on it that the officer behind me should be able to blend in too.

I walked slowly, soaking it all in. Once or twice, I stopped to look around and glance discreetly behind me. Every time, the man in jeans and a T-shirt was somewhere behind me. I turned onto Main Street. I was just a couple of blocks down from the café. I figured I'd walk by there, poke my head in to make sure Rhonda was doing okay, and then continue on towards the beach. It felt good to be out in the world.

I stopped to look in a shop window and checked behind me again. I couldn't see the officer, but I told myself he was back there. Main Street was busier than the side streets had been, so he was probably just hidden behind someone else.

I kept going. I was getting closer to the café now. The building Sammy lived in was just behind me. I passed a narrow alleyway that held the fire escape for one of the apartments in the building next to Sammy's. Latte's ears perked up as he heard a dog barking somewhere on the other side of the street. I turned my head to look just as someone grabbed me from behind and pulled me into the alley.

I tried to scream, but a cloth covered my mouth. My attacker's forearm pressed against my throat as they dragged me back. I kicked backward, trying for the shins of the person holding me. I only got air, and my feet slipped out from under me.

There was something on the cloth that burned

my nose. I shook my head to try to break free. They yanked back again. I felt like I was choking.

Latte barked and growled. The pressure against my throat disappeared, and Latte's leash wrenched out of my hand. His barking got quieter as he ran off, leaving me to my attacker. Where was the officer who was following me? I scratched at the arm as it went back around my throat. I had to stay in the alley. I had to stop them from dragging me into the parking lot behind it. I had to stay. I had to fight. Just until the officer caught up to me.

The hand over my mouth shifted, and the cloth covered my nose as well. I shook my head, trying to get away from the cloth. The hand clamped down tighter. I kicked the air. I tried to claw at the arm again, but my arm was heavy—too heavy to lift. I kicked again, but this time my leg stayed on the ground. The world swirled around me. I fought for consciousness. I couldn't pass out. I couldn't. I had to stay awake, had to stay here. Like in a dream, I felt my body start to sink. I tried to stand up, but the ground felt like water. A gray cloud moved into my vision. The world shrank to a tiny dot.

Latte was barking. I could hear him in the distance, or maybe not the distance. Maybe he was right beside me. Maybe he wasn't there at all. I imagined I heard footsteps running and a shout. A thud. The ground fell out from under me, and I landed on the pavement. The world started to grow again. Someone somewhere shouted my name. Latte barked. A figure appeared above me, and I fought to focus my eyes.

"Fran! Fran! Fran!" the voice screamed above me. "Franny!" Slowly, the face came into focus. Blond hair and big blue eyes. Sammy. "Fran! Are you okay?" She held a cast-iron skillet in her hand.

My head rolled to the side. I blinked at the body on the ground next to me. My mouth tried to work, but my tongue was huge and dry, so the word came out thick and slurred. "Karli?"

Chapter 27

I SAT at my desk in the back room of the café, flipping through applications. I was back to having to hire a new employee. I'd posted the barista job again and had a whole new stack of resumes, most of them only marginally more qualified than the batch that included Ephy's. Pretty much anyone halfway decent was only looking for seasonal work, and while I needed that, I needed someone during the off season too. Maybe a qualified person would just walk through the door, and I wouldn't have to worry about it anymore.

The door opened. Sammy poked her head through and smiled. "The boys are here," she said.

"I'll be right there." I stuffed the applications in a folder and put it in my top desk drawer. I could worry about them tomorrow. Tonight, we were closing early.

I ran my fingers through my hair and touched up my lipstick in the mirror then grabbed the heavy tote bag from under the desk. I slung my purse over my shoulder and went out to the front.

"Everybody ready?" Ryan asked from where he and Sammy were standing by the door.

"Ready!" I said.

Matt grabbed me around the waist and kissed me on the lips.

I grinned when he pulled away. "Nice lipstick."

He wiped at his mouth with the back of his hand and blushed when he saw the red streaks across it. I grabbed a handful of napkins and tried to help, but at some point it was impossible to tell the difference between the lipstick and the redness that came from rubbing the lipstick off. "At least they'll all know I'm taken," he said in a low voice that gave me shivers. I loved him so much.

Ryan held the door for us, and then I locked up. Our little group started the short walk to Cape Bay Town Hall.

Sammy grabbed my hand as we passed the alleyway where Karli had attacked me. "I still can't believe she tried to kill you," she whispered.

"I still can't believe you whacked her over the head with a cast-iron skillet," I replied.

She giggled. "It was such good luck that I forgot the skillet and came back for it."

"No kidding!"

"I don't understand why she wanted to kill you. It was really just because she thought you had a thing for Todd?" Ryan asked.

I shrugged. "That's my understanding. It doesn't make sense to me, but I guess it made sense to her."

"You were never even alone together," Matt said. "Were you?"

I elbowed him in the ribs. "No, of course not. And even if we had been, we're both happy with our partners. *Were* happy, I guess."

I'd run into Todd a couple of times since Karli's arrest—once at the grocery store and a couple of times at his gym, where I was still taking classes. The first time, he'd tried to stammer an apology for Karli, but he looked so stricken that I told him it wasn't his fault.

It wasn't, of course. He'd had nothing to do with her poisoning the punch or the chocolates or trying to chloroform me to death, but he knew that she was doing it because she wanted to keep him.

From what Mike said, she'd told Todd as much when she was being guarded in the hospital while she recovered from the concussion Sammy gave her. As far as I knew, she never said what it was that made her think I wanted Todd or that he would even consider leaving her for me, but that was what she thought, which was why she was facing dozens of charges for assault, murder, and attempted murder.

I was relieved that I could feel safe again, but I was sad too. She was so young. It was such a waste of a life.

Mike greeted us at the door to Town Hall and escorted us up to the council chambers. There were seats reserved for the four of us in the front row. When Sammy was looking the other way, I passed Mike the tote bag, and he disappeared up to the front with it.

We took our seats and talked quietly amongst ourselves until the meeting was called to order.

Sammy's recognition was the first thing on the agenda.

The mayor called us up to the front, where Sammy and I stood side by side with Ryan and Matt behind us.

"Samantha Ericksen," he began, "it is my privilege today to recognize you with the highest civilian award Cape Bay has to offer." There was some laughter, since that was also the only civilian award our small town had. The mayor continued. "The Cape Bay Mayor's Commendation in honor of your heroism in wielding a cast-iron skillet against an armed attacker and rescuing Francesca Amaro. We are truly proud to have you as a daughter of Cape Bay."

The small crowd made up mostly of our friends applauded as the mayor handed Sammy a framed certificate.

"I understand there's something else?" The mayor looked around.

Mike stepped forward with the cast-iron skillet I'd slipped to him earlier. He passed it to the mayor.

"Is this *the* skillet?" he asked. He weighed it in his hands to demonstrate its heft to the audience. The mayor had a reputation for being a bit of a ham when given the opportunity. "Impressive! Did you use one hand or two?"

Sammy flushed bright red. "Two."

He held it like a baseball bat in front of him and mocked a swing. "Yes, I can see how that would work better." His demonstration done, he reverted to a slightly more dignified manner. "Now, Sammy, something you don't know is that your friends had a little work done on this skillet for you."

She looked at me. I smiled and shrugged. I'd just gotten the skillet back from the local metalsmith that morning. I knew what he'd done, but she didn't.

The mayor turned the skillet over in his hands so that the back was facing the public. "It's engraved. Can you all read what this says? It says Sammy's Sledgehammer, and it has the date right here that she saved Fran. Let's all give Sammy a round of applause!"

The townspeople clapped for Sammy. Ryan and Matt contributed a little gratuitous cheering that soon spread until everyone was on their feet, applauding Sammy.

We both had tears in our eyes as she turned to hug me. "Thank you," I whispered.

"People will know better than to mess with us again," she whispered back.

"I sure hope so." I hugged her tight, feeling safe and blissfully happy. Everything was right with the world. Except for the sticky issue that I still had to hire more staff.

Recipe 1: Cream Horns

Makes 16-18 cream horns

Ingredients:
- 1 pack puff pastry sheets
- Cream horn molds

Cream ingredients:
- 8 oz. whipped topping, thawed
- 8 oz. cream cheese, room temperature
- $\frac{1}{2}$ cup powdered sugar

Preheat oven to 400°F. Roll out each sheet of dough into a square on a surface dusted with flour. Cut dough into $\frac{3}{4}$-inch-wide strips. Wrap each strip around the cream horn mold, overlapping so there are no gaps.

Place them on a greased pan or baking sheet. Bake for 18 minutes or until light golden brown. Remove from oven. Using gloves or a towel to hold the ends of the mold so you don't burn your hands, remove each horn from the mold to prevent them from sticking together. Let horn cool completely before filling with cream.

For Cream:

Beat Cool Whip and cream cheese in a medium bowl until well combined. Add powdered sugar and increase mixer speed until combined and smooth in texture.

Fill a decorating bag with cream mixture, using a size-appropriate attachment to squeeze the cream into the horns. Pipe cream into each horn.

Recipe 2: Shortbread Cookies

Ingredients:

- 1 cup butter, softened
- $\frac{1}{2}$ cup icing sugar
- $\frac{1}{2}$ cup cornstarch
- 1 pinch salt
- 2 cups all-purpose flour

Preheat oven to 325°F. In a medium bowl, beat butter for about 3 minutes, until cream. Sift in icing sugar, cornstarch, salt, and flour. It's better to do this in four parts, using a wooden spoon to mix in ingredients in between. Knead.

Roll dough onto a surface dusted with flour, with a rolling pin dusted with flour. Roll to desired thickness and cut using the cookie cutters of your choice. Place on a cookie sheet. Bake for 10-12 minutes, but don't let cookies get brown. Let cool on rack before moving them to a wire rack.

Recipe 3: Raspberry Punch

Ingredients:
- 1/2 gallon **raspberry sherbet**
- 2 liters **lemon-lime soda**
- 4 cups **pineapple juice**
- Optional: fresh or frozen raspberries for garnish

In a large punch bowl, add half of the sherbet and all of the soda and juice. Stir the sherbet with a wooden spoon until it combines with the liquid. Scoop out balls of the rest of the sherbet and include in the punch. Garnish with berries if desired.

About the Author

Harper Lin is a *USA TODAY* bestselling cozy mystery author.

When she's not reading or writing, she loves hiking, doing yoga, and hanging out with her family and friends.

For a complete list of her books by series, visit her website.

www.HarperLin.com

Made in the USA
Coppell, TX
26 August 2021